EDNA
THE INEBRIATE WOMAN

EDNA

THE INEBRIATE WOMAN

by

JEREMY SANDFORD

Marion Boyars
London

A MARION BOYARS BOOK
distributed by
Calder and Boyars Ltd.
18 Brewer Street, London W1R 4AS

This screenplay was first published in Great Britain in 1976
by Marion Boyars Publishers Ltd
18 Brewer Street, London, W1R 4AS

© Jeremy Sandford

All performing rights in this screenplay are strictly reserved
and application for performances should be made to
Nicholas Thompson Limited
83 Queen's Gate, London SW7 5JX.

Typesetting by Gilbert Composing Services,
Leighton Buzzard, Beds.

Printed by Unwin Brothers Limited,
Gresham Press, Old Woking, Surrey.
A member of the Staples Printing Group.

CONTENTS

INTRODUCTION

Edna was written because of my anger at the sort of lives that we, an affluent country, are prepared to tolerate for those in the bilges of our population.

In *Cathy* I had written of the cruelty done to our homeless families. Now I wanted to look at the lives of our *single* homeless—the sort of person that Cathy had become, when, stripped of her family, she walked into the night away from the railway station.

Specific impetus was given by the Rev. Ian Henderson of the Christian Action Hostel for Homeless Women in Lambeth High Street, and I kept in close touch with and received much help from the staff and clients of the hostel.

The response of society to the single homeless is, I believe, both absurd and expensive.

We send them on a trek from prison to psychiatric hospital, to common lodging house, which does nothing to help them and is immensely expensive to the taxpayer.

How many people are there like Edna in Britain? And what attitude should we take to them? At the time when *Edna* was first written, concern about the homeless family had been mobilised in 'Shelter' and the Squatters, but the equally grave problem of homeless single persons had so far received less attention. Such people are often dubbed 'socially inadequate', and information about them was fairly hard to come by.

Kenneth Stonely, representing the National Association of Voluntary Hostels, an organisation that tries to find homes for such people, told me, 'We alone now try to find homes for thousands of such people each year. Some thousands sleep out. Others will come from a meagre bed in a common lodging house (about 30,000 beds in Britain) or a psychiatric hospital, or prison, or some other type of institution.' These are the exits from the down-and-out world. The fruitless heavens for those who've fallen foul of 'Britain basking in its contemporary affluence'.

Anton Wallich-Clifford of the Simon Community Trust has campaigned through most of his life for such people. He said, 'The Survey done by the National Assistance Board in 1966 estimated many thousands of people who sometimes or habitually sleep rough. My researches indicate an even greater number. To the thousands of people in reception centres and common lodging houses must be added thousands of homeless inadequate single people who are, at the moment, in mental hospitals or prison or other institutions. The homeless single person—who is he? So often he is someone who has suffered a series of acts of violence which have been directed against him. I estimate there are in Britain 100,000 people of this type for whom there are no social services available from which they could get real benefit. We at the Simon Community Trust have set up many hostels to try to help these people. I am hopeful—but also sometimes feel despair. Even in Brighton in February, so a survey showed, there were at least fifty people sleeping out—some in pleasure shelters overlooking the waves.'

'What makes them like they are?' I asked a doctor.

'Some claim it's very simple—and sad. That hardly any of them had the pleasure of a loving relationship with their parents. This is what maims them, so that they can't now make contact with society. Many others had foster parents. Others again were institutionalised in psychiatric hospital or prison.'

Christian Action has established a hostel for such people and describes them in a handout, written by Leslie Tuft, as follows: 'Many live in shiftless existence, moving restlessly from one lodging house to another. Others are to be found in psychiatric and general hospitals, casualty departments, police stations, and in prison. Yet others have no alternative but to sleep rough in doorways or all-night launderettes, telephone kiosks, on the wooden benches of the main-line railway stations. Traumatic childhood experiences, early departure from the family home, loss of family ties, inability to settle for long in one job or one place, no marriage or a disastrous failure of marriage, all contribute to the development of a possible social isolation.'

I arranged in the script for Edna to pass through many of the traditional lodging places of persons of her type. Sometimes she was sleeping out in 'derries' (derelict buildings). Occasionally she used the 'Spike'—or reception centre. These places are so named because in the old days, in exchange for a night's shelter, you had to break up a certain number of rocks on a spike. There used to be Spikes arranged as a network all over Britain, usually connected to the old workhouses, and each a day's walk apart. Since the war, however, the policy has been to close them down, so that there are not many of them left now and they've been renamed 'Reception Centres'.

A rung above these again come the 'kiphouses'. Many of these are run by the Salvation Army, some run by local authorities, others by Rowton Houses, the Church Army, and others. Beyond these are psychiatric hospital and prison.

The events of my story of Edna are all based on real events that happened to real down-and-outs—men and women—within the last few years.

Move on, move on. This seems to be the reality of life for thousands of dossers and down-and-outs in Britain.

'Oh yes, the shades (police) like to have a clean beat,' one tells me. And yet down-and-outs possess many Christ-like virtues. They take no thought for the morrow, lay up no worldly goods.

People like Edna are people to whom violence has been done. And to a certain extent this has kept them, though adult in physical appearance, at the stage of development of children.

If I behave unjustly to a child he will sulk and say, 'I hate you'. But what he is really saying is, 'Please love me'. A wise parent or schoolmaster realises this, and that a fit of the sulks, accompanied by', Fuck society, put me back in the nick, at any rate that's warm,' etc. etc., is a plea for help.

Help we must and care we must. More and more
people each year are going into care, and, despite
pruning, entry into psychiatric hospitals remains
roughly constant. More people are going into the
courts, into homes for juveniles and into prison—
especially teenagers.

The flood of homeless teenagers who seem unable
to cope with society is becoming so great that it
now constitutes one-third of all the NAVH
placements. And this is a grave sign. Many of course
will find a happier orientation in life when they
'settle down'. But the numbers are too great for us
to write off the danger so easily.

And, if we don't learn better how to cope with
the Ednas of Britain they will continue to grow in
numbers—until they constitute a population
numbering, not one hundred thousand, but
hundreds of thousands.

I believe that the answer for Britain's thousands of
Ednas' lies in permissive hostels akin to the fictional
one run by Josie in my script. Hostels like this that
I have been connected with and applaud are run by
the Cyrenians. There are too many people around
who are not capable of functioning outside a
protective set-up. But, once provide that protective
set-up, which need be little more than a house that
they can be confident they'll not be thrown out of,
and these people can achieve a happy and fulfilled
life. Those considering what life-style would be
most fulfilling for themselves and also helpful to
others could do worse than consider going through
the necessary stages to set up such a place. Most
people make the decision to have a family and look

after their own children. But there is a need for hundreds of people to make a different decision, and, instead, set up artificial families.

This is happening. All the time, new hostels or 'houses of hospitality' are springing up and there are now hundreds of places in Britain corresponding more or less to the one run by Josie in this script. But the situation is not a rosy one. There have also been many closures. Many people in this field of social work have told me that pressure gets worse, not better. There is need for hundreds more. What threatens this sort of hostel?

Firstly, the problem of personnel. It is hard to find someone of the right personality to run them.

Secondly, finance. The Government can underpin the price of beds for certain types of hostel. This is good. Some hostels, however, are run on such a shoestring that it is impossible for them to get up to the standards which would be passable by the local Health Inspector. Receiving Government money would make them liable to be inspected and so they do not claim money because they fear that if they were inspected they would be closed down.

In those hostels which are not afraid of this, one of the most important things that a kindly person running them can do is to help their residents claim what is their right from Social Security. So often a failure in communication has resulted in a breakdown in relationships with the Social Security and this can be put right. The Social Security will then pay their rent.

A few local authorities are making available houses which are not to be developed for a few years to those who would like to run houses of hospitality. Otherwise it is necessary to find such a place to rent or to buy—this again presents money problems.

A third thing which threatens the establishment of hostels is the antagonism of neighbours. Here there is a need for greater understanding. And I would be happy if I felt that Edna had helped a little with this.

Jeremy Sandford

CREDITS

Written by	Jeremy Sandford
Director	Ted Kotcheff
Photography	Peter Bartlett
Sound	Peter Edwards
Editor	Peter Coulson
Producer	Irene Shubik

Edna, the Inebriate Woman was written in late 1968 and early 1969. It was filmed by Ted Kotcheff for the BBC and transmitted in 1971.

This version of the script is the one from which the film was made, (BBC project no. 02140/3484). I have tidied it up in places to make it easier reading. I have added two scenes that I wrote, at Ted Kotcheff's suggestion, while the film was being made. These are the 'Blimey O'Reilly' scene in the dormitory at the spike, and the scene in the washroom at the 'Manor House'.

CAST

EDNA	Patricia Hayes
JOSIE	Barbara Jefford
IRENE	Patricia Nye
ATTENDANT AT THE SPIKE . .	June Watson
DOCTOR AT THE SPIKE . . .	Denis Carey
OLD MEN	Gerry Verno
	Rex Rashley
PROPRIETOR OF COMMON	
LODGING HOUSE	Walter Sparrow
JESSIS	Amelia Bayntun
SOCIAL SECURITY CLERK . .	Douglas Ditta
TRAMPS	Chris Gannon
	Talfryn Thomas
	Charles Farrell
	Vivian Macherrell
PADDY AT COMMON LODGING	
HOUSE	Marie Conmee
DORIS, ON THE ROAD	Jenny Logan
MAN IN CAR	Anthony Dawes
SOCIAL SECURITY OFFICIAL .	Elaine Mitchell
PSYCHIATRIST	John Hussey
OLD WOMEN	Dorothy Lane
	Patsy O'Shea
CLARA	June Brown
STAFF NURSE	Jumoke Derayo
NINA	Jo Maxwell Muller
PSYCHIATRIST IN HOSPITAL . .	Malcolm Terris
PORTER	Keith Marsh
PROPRIETOR OF LODGING	
HOUSE	Eamonn Boyce
ROGO AT CHARITABLE	
INSTITUTION	James Cairncross
BED TICKET PROPRIETOR . .	Virginia Snyders
SOCIAL SECURITY CLERK . .	Alex Marshall

MAGISTRATE	Norman Lumsden
POLICEMAN	Mark Moss
NUNS	Merelina Kendall
	Francis Tomelty
MOTHER SUPERIOR	Freda Dowie
GRAHAM	John Trigger
TRUDI	Geraldine Sherman
VANGI	Cheryl Hall
TERESA	Kate Williams
VICTOR	Roger Hammond
LIL	Peggy Aitchison
COUNSEL AT PUBLIC HEARING .	Jeffrey Sega
DEFENCE	David Garth
CHAIRMAN	George Belbin

The author acknowledges, with much gratitude, the splendour of Patricia Hayes' performance as Edna, and the magnificence of Ted Kotcheff's direction.

EDNA THE INEBRIATE WOMAN

screenplay

A Road. Night

*Out of the darkness, out of the night, a frayed
decrepit fragile old figure emerges.*

*First she is a speck lit up fitfully by the headlamps
of passing cars. Then she gets closer and we see her
solitary trudge. Under one arm she has a polythene
parcel. She passes us and continues.*

Common Lodging House. Kitchen. Night

Tatty room with two or three gas stoves in it.

EDNA *a curious bundle of rags, is leaping up and
down on the floor of the kitchen, a bizarre figure,
trying to stamp on beetles.*

*She stops to turn on the gas for a cup of tea, then
returns to her occupation.*

PROPRIETOR.   Out you go Edna now, you know you
can't stay here—we're closed. Haven't I told you
that?

EDNA.   Sorry. Sorry. I was just trying to rid it of the
beetle. After so many beetle . . .

PROPRIETOR.   Never mind the beetle. Anyway, they
won't harm you no more. You're going. Remember?

EDNA.   I was just trying to stamp out the beetle.

PROPRIETOR.   Why?

21

EDNA. Cos I don't like them.

PROPRIETOR. They won't worry you. You're going. Edna. (*hustling her*) Remember? G-O-I-N-G spells going.

EDNA. Goodbye. Goodbye beetle.

EDNA *leaves.*

On the Road. Night

EDNA *walking. She mutters.*

EDNA. After so many. After so many beetle.

A tree is lit up fitfully by the headlamps of a passing car.

EDNA. Life . . . I call it a study in dry rot. Flitter. Flitter.

As she trudges we hear

OFFICIAL VOICE. Some of the inmates of the lodging house took it badly. Two of them even went out and threw a brick through a window.

EDNA. But I didn't do it. Oh no, I didn't do it. No. Flitter. Flitter

In a Ruined Building in the Country. Night

EDNA *sitting by a very small fire.*
She explains to an OLD TRAMP

EDNA. It's me legs, see, it's me legs. Yes, it's me legs play me up. In the summer, in the summer things are much better. It's the while we have all this cold, that's the trouble, that's when me legs go numb with an awful lot of pain . . . Well, like today, there was a little bit of sun, I went and sat in the sun and I felt a great improvement. As long as it

22

don't get too hot. But it don't do that this time of
the year. Too much hot draws it. Worse than the
other. But we should be all right now. Well, sometimes the sun draws them sometimes it's the cold
draws them, draws me veins you see.

Spike. Night

*A metal door in which there is a small grill. The little
panel behind the grill opens and* ATTENDANT's *face
peers out. The panel closes and door opens.* EDNA
enters.

Spike Hallway. Night

FEMALE SPIKE ATTENDANT.   Name?

EDNA.   Edna O'Casey

ATTENDANT.   Let's see your cards

EDNA.   Ain't got no cards

ATTENDANT.   Sorry, you can't come here if you've
got no cards.

EDNA.   I can. You've got to take me in. It's me right

ATTENDANT.   Sod your right. No cards and you don't
come in here. Any other way of identifying
yourself?

EDNA.   I've got a right to come here and I've a right to
put right me right to putting me right foot; sock
you in the ear'ole!

ATTENDANT.   Sod off.

Spike. Bath-house. Night

EDNA *naked. Being inspected by* ATTENDANT *with
the aid of a small portable searchlight.*

ATTENDANT.   Where are you from?

EDNA. From around. From round about. Just from the round about.

ATTENDANT. Yes, but before you got to the roundabout.

EDNA *shyly in the form of a small question;*

EDNA. I was in the Psychiatric? No, I been roundabout. Just from round about the rounds—the roundabout.

ATTENDANT. *Sighs.* You used to be on the road once long ago wasn't you? Always popping in from some different direction?

EDNA. Yes. I used to be on the road at one time. But now I'm more settled down. (*pause*) In regular work. Why have they moved this place? It used to be in the centre of the town.

ATTENDANT. Administrative difficulties.

EDNA. They moved it because they want to stamp out us people. Stamp us off the earth.

ATTENDANT. It was thought to be better to put it here.

EDNA *moves to bathe herself.*

The ATTENDANT *now searches her clothing for nits and lice with the same powerful searchlight.*

During her search she comes across a half bottle of V.P. wine, which she throws into a dustbin.

ATTENDANT. Are you sure you're skint? You know you have to be skint to come here.

EDNA *in shower or bath, says:*

EDNA. I'm sure.

ATTENDANT. I know you say you're sure, but are you really?

24

EDNA. Yes.

ATTENDANT. Well, you know you'll have to leave
   tomorrow.

EDNA. Yes.

The ATTENDANT *places* EDNA*'s clothing in a
strong polythene bag and adds ethyl formate to it.*

ATTENDANT. I'll have to de-infestate these clothes.
   Here you are.

She hands EDNA *a coarse nightdress.*

Spike. Dining-room. Night

There are ten tables.

Silence

EDNA *sitting eating a large hunk of bread, corned
beef, a large cup of tea.*

A WOMAN *sits to whom* EDNA *talks.*

EDNA. An old fella tells me the other day; I've given
   up gambling and I've given up drinking and swearing.
   Bloody 'ell, says he, I've left me playing cards
   down the pub.

EDNA *laughs. She looks at the* WOMAN *hoping
for some reaction.*

But there is none.

Spike. The Dormitory. Night

Silence

EDNA *finishes taking off top clothes and is
getting into bed.*

Twenty beds. A few occupied.

EDNA *gets into bed and lies down.*

WOMAN.   Lie down. Lie down. Come on chicken.

    EDNA *sits up.*

EDNA.   What did you say?

WOMAN.   Lie down! Blimey O'Reilly. Don't know where you're going or what you're doing! Lie down! Now here. Now there. This place isn't the bloody beach you know.

EDNA.   I'm sorry.

    EDNA *lies down.*

WOMAN.   I saw you. Lie down. And go to sleep. Blimey O'Reilly. Awake half the night.

    EDNA *sits up.*

EDNA.   Shut up.

    She lies down again.

WOMAN.   Taking it easy. This place isn't the beach you know.

Spike. A Room

A bench on which sit OLD MEN *and* EDNA

DOCTOR.   Are you in work now?

OLD MAN I.   Oh, yes, sir.

DOCTOR   What are you doing?

OLD MAN I.   I'm doing the buckets and that outside the bathroom. And swilling down the tiles.

    The DOCTOR *sits at a green baize covered table.*

    A fire is burning brightly.

DOCTOR.   Oh, so you work *here.*

OLD MAN I.   Yes

DOCTOR.   Did you ever try for work outside?

OLD MAN I.   Yes sir.

DOCTOR.   Where?

OLD MAN I.   Yes sir.

DOCTOR.   How did they treat you at the Social
Security?

OLD MAN I.   No, sir.

DOCTOR.   What. They didn't treat you well?

OLD MAN I.   No, sir.

DOCTOR.   Did they suggest you get work?

OLD MAN I.   No, sir.

DOCTOR *listens hopefully.*

OLD MAN I.   Said I was too old.

DOCTOR.   Did they go by how old you are, or how
old you look?

OLD MAN I.   Sir, don't know sir.

DOCTOR.   Would you like to stay here inside through
the winter?

OLD MAN I.   Oh, yes, sir.

Pause. Looks at books and at his ASSISTANT
for any possible objections.

DOCTOR.   All right. We'll let you stay here through
the winter and then turn you out in the summer.
That all right?

A smile of joy lights up the OLD MAN's *face.*

OLD MAN I.   We thank you sir!

The OLD MAN *goes.*

ASSISTANT *beckons brusquely to the next*
OLD MAN. *The* OLD MAN *comes over.*

The ASSISTANT *is a man about fifty. He is
dressed in a white lab coat.*

DOCTOR.   You're almost the oldest inhabitant?

OLD MAN II.   Sorry, sir.

DOCTOR. *shouting*   I think you're about the oldest
inhabitant?

OLD MAN II.   I *can* hear what you're saying, sir. I
can hear what you're saying. I *can* hear what you
you're saying, sir.

DOCTOR. *shouts.*   I said, you're almost the oldest
inhabitant here!

OLD MAN II.   Oh, No, sir. Yes, sir, yes, sir. No sir!

DOCTOR. *aside.*   Oh, yes. I remember. He worked
in an ammunition factory, didn't he, and it blew
up, and he didn't get a pension.

CUT TO:

MAN III *locked in his own particular silence.
The* DOCTOR *clutches him gently by the
shoulder and makes spade shovelling gestures and
then points at him questioningly.*

There is a pause, and then the OLD MAN *makes
vigorous boot-repairing gestures.*

ASSISTANT. *writing*   Deaf and Dumb

DOCTOR.   No, born deaf, hence dumb. He could speak
if he were taught.

CUT TO:

MAN IV *has black slightly thinning hair, black*

eyes protruding from pink lids.

MAN IV.   I've shrunk.   Dunno why.   I've shrunk.   I feel better when I'm drunk.

DOCTOR.   Weren't you light-weight champion for England once?

MAN IV.   Oh yes.

His face lights up.

EDNA.   Please sir.

EDNA appears at the door.

She stands, wringing her hands round her bit of polythene.

DOCTOR.   Yes?

EDNA.   Can you take me in, sir? Can I be tachy to the house? Can you take me in for the winter? And something for a cough. And I want to complain about the dreams I've been getting. Terrible dreams.

DOCTOR.   Oh, Edna! Oh dear, we've nowhere for you! I'm sorry, Edna. They're closing down all the beds in the women's wing. Except for the one-night casuals. I'm sorry. *(Gently)*. I would take you in if I could, dear.

EDNA.   Thank you very much sir.

She goes.

Gothic passage in the Spike

EDNA *and* OLD WOMAN II *sit on bench.*

EDNA.   Look what I've found.

OLD WOMAN II.   You can't smoke that in here.

EDNA.   It's only a fag end.

ASSISTANT *enters and* EDNA *hides the burning cigarette behind her. Smoke rises behind her.* ASSISTANT *exits:* EDNA *jumps, slaps her behind, trying to put out the fire.*

An Office

OFFICIAL I *sits behind a table.*

EDNA *has lifted her grubby lengthy skirts to show her boot to* OFFICIAL I.

She shows a booted foot, worn away through the sole.

OFFICIAL I.   Yes, I can see it is in a bad way.

EDNA.   I've been walking quite a bit, this one is through.

OFFICIAL I.   Yes. But, how do I know you don't have other pairs in your lodgings?

EDNA *triumphant.*   I ain't got no lodgings! I sleep out, don't I? I don't have no lodgings.

OFFICIAL I.   Could you come back and ask me again on Monday?

EDNA *smiles.*   If I'm around I'll come back. 'Tis only one boot. This one's all right.

OFFICIAL I *hardened, but also harassed.*   I'm sorry, not till—Listen, I do understand . You think I don't understand, but I do. You need money, accommodation. You need a decent job. I know about you. You need decent clothes. I know all about you really, and I do understand. Listen Miss, er—I've got fifty people on my books. . . all right. I'll give you a coat.

On the Road

EDNA, *walking, in the overcoat. Her face, wrinkled,*

bears the marks of decades of grime. She wears no socks, boots, an assortment of dingy, ill-fitting, flapping clothes. A pork-pie hat stuffed down over her head.

She looks about seventy-five but is not, and peers out at the world through moist and luminous eyes. She is sexless—could be man or woman.

She is walking doggedly along the road.

EDNA.   I haven't had a meal since yesterday. I didn't have a meal today. *Pause.* I kept going on apples. I am on the tramp all night and I've kept on tramping after the day has broken. And I've kept on tramping.

Now she passes through a small market town, surrounded by a wide expanse of common land.

Chimneys of working-class houses issuing bluey-white smoke.

A working-class cafe: MEN *having breakfast.*

EDNA.   People are getting up, the cafes are opening. You can smell the breakfasts. And I ain't got any money to buy me breakfast.

She climbs down to a stream and drinks from her hat.

Police car passes over bridge above EDNA, *slows down a moment, then moves on.*

The voice of EDNA;

EDNA.   You can't stop. The shades won't let you. You go on. So you say, all right, I'll go on. So you got a target. So you go on, you say, I'll go on to the next town. And from there—it's only

a short step back home to where you come from.

By the stream, she spies potatoes growing and goes and roots one up.

A MOTHER *waves her* CHILDREN *off to school.*

A tall blank brick wall with a single door.

A notice on the door says: No Beds. It is chalked on cardboard.

TWO OLD WOMEN *are waiting outside—but largely indistinguishable from men.*

EDNA *approaches.*

EDNA.   They got any beds?

JESSIE.   I don't know.

EDNA.   What's it like in there?

JESSIE.   Cold.

Pause

The side of JESSIE's *mouth twists for a moment into a grin.*

JESSIE.   You know anyone would care to publish some drawings?

EDNA.   No, dear.

JESSIE   I had a portfolio once. Full of drawings.

EDNA.   You got it still, dear? *Ritually, she knows the answer*

JESSIE.   No. Somebody whipped it.

EDNA.   Will they take you in without money?

33

A momentary wry grin, then JESSIE *looks at her again from her piercing eyes.*

JESSIE. How would they take you in without money?

JAMIE *an Irishman, joins the group.*

JAMIE. Any beds guv?

EDNA. *cheerfully* No beds. I think.

JAMIE. Where do you sleep if there's no beds here?

JESSIE. In the ruined derries down the road. That's where we do our skipper.

EDNA. *sympathetic.* Are you down?

JAMIE. Well, yes.

EDNA. There's many things pull you down. Many come of good stock, but now they're down. Sometimes the nerves. Sometimes its family trouble. Sometimes money worries.

JAMIE. *absently* Yes, yes. That's right. *Then, matter of fact.* Where is these places for a skipper then?

EDNA. Down the road. Down there. *Cheerfully.* They call it the road to nowhere.

JAMIE. I'm under psychiatric treatment actually.

JAMIE *shows* EDNA *a card.*

He reads aloud;

JAMIE. Winterbourne Psychiatric Hospital. Would you care to see my hospital?

EDNA. All right, I'll view the premises.

On the Road

EDNA *is tramping with* JESSIE

EDNA.   Wayfaring is a very funny thing. Sometimes
you're happy in it and sometimes you're not.
You feel cut off. Do you find that?

JESSIE.   Oh yes.

EDNA.   It's not that I dislike people what is
settled. I watch them and wish I could be same
as them.

By a Barn

EDNA *is sitting with* JESSIE.

EDNA.   I'll give you a word of advice. Go to
St. Gertrude's.

JESSIE.   St. Gertrude's? I've been many a time to
St. Gertrude's.

EDNA.   Well, they'll set you up! Like you know
dish scrapin', pot cleanin' uppin'. Get you a job.

JESSIE.   Did you do that?

EDNA.   I did. But I couldn't stick it. Oh no—so I
didn't stick it.

By a small fire in a Derelict Building. Night

EDNA *sits, drinks from a bottle of surgical spirits, with*
JESSIE.

EDNA.   Sometimes I think I once knew something
of very great importance. And other times I don't.
I'm in work. I'm in a very good job, matter of
fact. I've got a very good memory.

JESSIE.   Oh yes. I'm sure you're right. I'm in work too

35

same as you.

EDNA.   It's like I drank the tea and the tea-leaves as
well. I drank the tea-leaves so I don't no more like
the tea. And so, flitter . . . flitter . . . I learned
something about life, but I don't know how to tell
it. So I find it hard sometimes to talk. Oh, excuse . . .

*She coughs, rises, goes to a distance to cough. Lies
down, the better to contain it. Lies still, so as not
to disturb the cough . . .*

Later, before she falls asleep;

EDNA.   I like to sleep out. That's what keeps me in
good 'ealth.

*She wraps herself in newspapers, and in a blanket
from the polythene bag.*

JESSIE *beds down for the night.*

And EDNA *sleeps.*

*Room, F.13. At the Offices
of the Social Security*

CLERK.   Anyway, how did you lose it?

EDNA.   If I knew that, I wouldn't have lost it, would
I?

CLERK.   What colour was it?

EDNA.   Primrose and/or pink.

CLERK.   Yes, well, that is not the colour of the
allowance book in question.

EDNA.   I did report it last week, but not here.

CLERK. Yes well.

EDNA. I need a quid.

CLERK. I can't do anything can I Mrs. Morrison? The only place that could help you is Broadstreet.

EDNA. I can't get there can I?

CLERK. No well.

EDNA. I'm going upstairs for a grant—being in dire need.

Room F.17

EDNA *sits down with* OTHERS.

EDNA. I am in dire need.

CLERK. Please do not sit on this side if you have not given your name to the receptionist.

The London House Canteen

EDNA *at the service counter.*
An officious WOMAN *in grubby white overalls.*
She stretches out her hand with the ticket.

EDNA. Soup please.

ATTENDANT II. You can't have just soup.

EDNA. I only want soup.

ATTENDANT II. Your breakfast ticket is worth three soups.

EDNA. Yes.

ATTENDANT.   What do you mean, yes? Three soups
    or no soup?

EDNA.   Three soups.

She juggles the three soups back to a table.

EDNA *to Attendant.*   Thanks very much.

Derry II. A Cellar

EDNA *descending the stairs leading into the cellar.*

*There are steps missing. The bannister is being torn·
from it for firewood.*

A fire burns.

Dark FIGURES *huddle round it.* WOMEN *and* MEN.

Water runs down the walls.

People collect it in tins.

Bearded MAN III *is stirring up a disgusting looking
mess in a frying pan.*

*In a large tin some noxious stew made from vegetables
is cooking.*

MAN IV *is trying to grill bacon in the top of a tin
that formerly held Snowcem,*

*Pigeons go where they want through the smoky
atmosphere, picking up titbits.*

MAN I Irish Mick.   Eff—you.

MAN II.   Double F—you!

*And they continue to shout raggedly at each
other.*

Then one MAN *commits an act of assault upon his
friend.*

Double F—you, I'll get your f-stick from out your f-ing flies.

There is a violent struggle at the end of which a MAN's *flies are ripped open.*

EDNA *is watching.*

MAN III.   Come on, drop that bloody H-bomb afore winter comes.

MAN I.   Come on, drink, drink! A two bob bottle will keep you two days high and rot your guts up quicker than nothing.

He swigs.

EDNA *settles on her polythene bag between* MAN III *and* MAN IV.

MAN IV.   I'm an Irishman and I've been twenty-five years in this country, and out of that twenty-five years I've spent fifteen in prison, so when I came out of prison I'm not long out of prison I went to the probation place. So I went there for a little bit of clothing, but I couldn't get the clothing, so myself and my friend we come out of that. So anyway when we comes out of that they couldn't get no clothing for us so on the road we're asking—as a matter of fact we are begging for anyone to give us the price of a cup of tea. No go.

He continues to talk—the story has no ending.

MAN III.   That's Tiny Nick. He's one of the famousest characters around here. He says he's God. Tell them. Tell them. How d'you know you're God?

MAN I.   I was saying my prayers to the Lord. Found I was talking to meself.

MAN III.   When he sits on the toilet he shits on the floor. Why do you do that? Say why you do that?

MAN I.   God made the toilet so God can shit where he pleases.

HIPPY.   Stuff this up your nostril and sniff. It's happy gas. It's incredible.

Throwing capsule from her EDNA *says;*

EDNA.   You doing a skipper because you have to, or for a rave?

The HIPPY *has stuffed capsule up his nose and is swaying about.*

An OLD MAN, *who has been sleeping beneath newspapers awakes and surveys the* HIPPY *with amazement.*

EDNA *also watches.*

Later

They walk.

EDNA.   Does your mind get cloudy sometimes? All clouded up?

JAMIE.   Oh yes, mine does. I go round the doctor's for drugs, it don't help. I'm sick you see, I'm sick. There's many takes an interest in me, but it don't help. I let them down, you see. One tip I will give you. You got a friend?

EDNA.   Oh no. I did once. Not now no more.

JAMIE.   Yes, well once you lose 'em you won't get them back. Anyway, Nerves bad? Your nerves get bad? Phanyl is good for that. Phanyl, is good for the nerves. Especially for women. A fellow told me. Write it down if you got a pencil. Phanyl.

EDNA *gets a half loaf wrapped in newspaper from her pocket Stump of pencil from another pocket.*

Unwraps newspaper laboriously. Writes it down in large capitals on the newspaper.

JAMIE.   I take it meself. My mind gets cloudy. It gets so cloudy sometimes, I walk all the way to the North to clear it. Seven days it takes. And when I get there, I feel so fed up so I turns round and I walks back.

EDNA.   Are you a deserter?

JAMIE.   No.

EDNA.   Look like a deserter from the bloody army.

JAMIE.   No I'm not that, but it's very hard in this world to belong. Do you find that? M.P's find it all right but for the ordinary person it's hard. You're ostracised you are because you stand up and say true facts. That's what I say.

EDNA *hands* JAMIE *a mint.*

JAMIE.   I volunteered in the war. I was sent to Wales. I was in the cycling club. Oh yes, with the club I used to go everywhere, we went all over the place. And in the war, when we met up with other soldiers. I said to them don't. Do you like square bashing? Do you like fatigues? Don't. Don't. They'll tell you you can build roads, we'il put you on building the roads if that's on your conscience, but a concrete road is a road to take guns on, isn't it? So they said we're going to segregate you. So you can't spread the gospel of peace. So I said segregate me if you like. But what I'm saying is true facts.

Charitable Hostel

A choir sings to twenty odd decrepit DOSSERS *and*

42

TRAMPS *who sit on benches.*

VICAR.   And now, while we hand out your grub, another anthem from the Breakfast Choir.

MEN *cough and spit, imprecate, groan.*
LADIES *pass out sandwiches.*

EDNA *has received a paper parcel consisting of two cheese and margarine sandwiches.*

EDNA *eats it, then makes a fake package from bits of newspaper. She puts it down on the pew to her left.*

Keeping a wary eye on OTHERS, *a* NEIGHBOUR *of* EDNA's *reaches across and draws it to her.*

Avidly she opens it. Is disappointed.

EDNA *laughs.*

*Entrance Hall of the Manor
House Lodging House*

"Good cheap lodgings for women."

A Georgian House.

At a counter the MANAGER *is counting the take.*

EDNA *enters the lodging house below the level of the counter.*

IRENE.   O.K. say nothing, say nothing. Come on. It's 'no beds' but I can help you.

She clutches EDNA's *arm.*

EDNA *recoils from the drunken* OLD WOMAN, *who detects* EDNA's *hesitation and says;*

IRENE.   Nothing else! Say nothing. Come on. Say

43

nothing. I help you! Help a friend in trouble!
Nothing else! You think I'm a Les don't you?
Well, I'm not. Nothing else!

She continues across the room.

Taps EDNA, *friendly, on the stomach.*

IRENE.   You all right, Paddy. You come with me.

Lodging House Kitchen

There is an open fireplace where WOMEN *are cooking and many* WOMEN *sitting around.*

IRENE.   Now I cook you something nice.

PADDY.   You can't come here. Paddies only.

She turns away.

IRENE.   This *is* a Paddy.

PADDY.   Kitchen's closed.

IRENE.   I'll speak to the manager.

PADDY.   I *am* the manager.

IRENE.   Too bad. Paddies run that part. Too bad . Try
later. Hey, got an idea! You say you got no bed
ticket?

EDNA.   No I got no ticket at all.

IRENE.   You sleep under bed! I sleep on top of the
bed! You under the bed. All dark! No one see!
Yes, is better! Nothing else wanted! Nothing else!

EDNA.   Can I really sleep under the bed?

IRENE.   Yes! Yes!

EDNA.   What do you want in exchange?

44

IRENE. Nothing! Nothing else! Nothing! Nothing!

Seeing that the PADDIES *are looking elsewhere,*
IRENE *crosses to hearth and puts on pot, then
comes back.*

IRENE *produces photographs.*

IRENE. Yes—was my *husband*—they my *children*—that
was me man's *car*—Yes, that was me. That's me
elkhound. Took them with me own *camera.* Here
was me man's *speed-boat.*

EDNA. Was that you?

*She is looking at a picture of a beautiful young
girl.*

IRENE. Takes some sorting out don't it? I mean, quite
a change!

IRENE *smiles sadly, then hits her a playful blow in
the stomach.*

TWO WOMEN *fighting amongst themselves, one
falls over with a heavy clump.*

The Washroom—a strange vaulted place

As we see the mainly OLD LADIES *washing, we hear
the voice of;*

DORELIA. A true case of hardship—*all* pass the Buck,
in *all* my 100 letters to *bring* this to public eye
are *ignored.* All the *collusions;* lying and cheating
that got me *out* of my *former* home and others got
possession of my *beloved* clothes, furniture, even
jewellery,—*all* behind this case. Even the Secretary
of this Society, *without* my *knowledge* signed
affidavit so I was literally *dragged back* into this
one Crummy *Cold* Room—evicted *minus* a *Towel,*
or *toothbrush* even on *eviction date*—Even my *Bed*

Linen, Blankets, *all left in house.* I *had* to *make*
20 phone calls, to get my *Blankets,* via Mental
Health Welfare. Yet said M.H. Officer had gone
into County Court and made sure, very sure by her
statement to the C.C. Judge that, *I would lose my*
home. This HER SPEECH, took three hours for
her to say *before Judge* shouted "POSSESSION!"
M.H. Officer *then* proceeded to make *verbal*
arrangements with owner *when* I could be *sure*
to be evicted. May God forgive them *All. I never*
can. Have contemplated suicide due this often.

Collusion of Solicitors (one acting for *Plaintiff*
and one who at the bitter end refused to lift a
finger to *help me* hold on to my home) their
ghastly act as been duly registered to Home
Secretary, 113 Chancery Lane, W.C.2. But each
time I get all the photostat denials from there I
cry and *cry.* I know it's all been a *frame-up* I
loved my former home—these men (if you can
call them *that*) All 'greed' to take it away from
me. Once was *happy.*

Dormitory Manor House. Later

WOMEN *climbing into their various beds.*

About thirty beds in this room, bare paned windows.

EDNA *gets under* IRENE*'s bed.*

Then a torch is shining on her.

MANAGEMENT VOICE.   Come on. Out! Out!
    Come on. You. Out!

So EDNA *climbs out from under the bed.*

On the Road

Desolate countryside road.

EDNA *and* DORIS, *a girl of twenty-six.*

DORIS. Well I'm a half and half against my will dear, they turned me into that but I want to be just a girl.

EDNA. Eh? What? You're a half and half. But you want to be a woman? Takes some sorting out.

DORIS. I wasn't born half and half. I dresses and lives like a girl, but I'm half and half. My girlfriend, she got pregnant.

EDNA. Takes some sorting out, don't it?

She thinks, at great length, says;

EDNA. Getaway! Ha ha! You don't say!

DORIS. Tend to drink, though. People tell me I'm likeable. Legally—well, legally—you know—

She puts her arm round EDNA.

DORIS. They took me into the psychiatric. They cut me breasts off. *(Then she says wonderingly)* Me breasts. Me breasts. Oh well, no good crying over spilt milk.

EDNA. Get away!

Then she decides that DORIS *must have made a joke and laughs. A car approaches. Stops.*

MAN. Can you tell me the way to Torrington?

DORIS. Torrington. Yes, I can show you. Can you give us a lift there?

MAN *looks horrified.*

EDNA. I'll tell you, I've been in the most roughest places. And at the same time I been in the best places.

MAN. I can see that.

DORIS. I know my hair is lovely. But underneath it's filled with nits. Excuse me , can you spare half a quid, sir? For a good time with two naughty girls?

The Offices of the Social Security

A long shot: A YOUNG MAN *reads The Evening Standard in the foreground. Headline:*

Get rid of the scroungers.

In background a long table with three INTERVIEWERS *and three* INTERVIEWEES, *one of which is* EDNA.

Benches with OTHERS *waiting.*

OFFICIAL II (a woman). The last amount we advanced you was as a result of your being in dire need. But— we can't continue to make these payments while you remain a vagrant—

EDNA. While I remain a what?

OFFICIAL II. While you remain a vagrant.

EDNA. The vagrant. I am not the vagrant! I'm not I'm not I'm not the vagrant. And I want money! I want money! I need money!

OFFICIAL II. Please lower your voice, madam, or I may have to take appropriate—

EDNA. All right, send for the bloody old shades! And

shut up! This has happened before! Listen, keep your bloody old money! I tell you, I may be the vagrant, but I am. I'm not the bloody old—

She hurls a blotting paper at the OFFICIAL, *knocks her chair over.*

Magistrate's Court

SOLICITOR FOR THE PROSECUTION. She was causing a disturbance in the Offices of the Social Security.

MAGISTRATE. Can you speak up, please? I can't hear you very well.

PROSECUTION. She was causing a disturbance in the Offices of the Social Security.

EDNA. No I was not sir, no I was not!

OTHERS. Shhh!

EDNA. I was just putting me point of view 'cos they called me the vagrant!

Psychiatrist's Office

EDNA *and* PSYCHIATRIST.

PSYCHIATRIST *sits at desk, has form in front of him.*

PSYCHIATRIST. The Magistrate referred you to me as you know. For a psychiatric report.

EDNA. They called me the vagrant. I am not the vagrant. I'm just the person wants to live their own life and go on me own little ways.

PSYCHIATRIST. Well, either I write here you're

49

disturbed and recommend you be admitted to our psychiatric hospital or I say that you're sane and send you back to Court for them to deal with you as they think fit. Which would *you* like?

Corridors. Psychiatric Hospital

EDNA *goes along the long corridors, walking the same way as she does along the roads.*

The Ward. Psychiatric Hospital

EDNA *is in a locked ward, which basically is a large space, one end of which, with little tables, is the dining-room. The other end contains easy chairs and a telly.*

WOMEN, *mainly young, wander here aimlessly, or sit in the easy chairs, or hover about the tables in the cafe.*

One hovers about like a bird, occasionally makes a diving leap down to pick up a piece of cigarette paper or part of a cigarette packet off the floor.

A youngish WOMAN *with her cardigan over her head glowers and hisses at* EDNA.

ANOTHER, *stands, arms folded, lost, hunched into herself.*

ANOTHER, *sits, silently laughing.*

Dining-room Section

EDNA *goes up to a table, where sit three* OLD WOMEN.

OLD WOMAN.   That seat's taken. Sorry.

   EDNA *goes to another table.*

OLD WOMAN.   That seat's taken. Sorry.

EDNA.   Oh.

OLD WOMAN.   You can sit over there though.

She points out an empty table, where EDNA *goes and sits.*

EDNA.   It's no good. I won't eat it. I only eat fish.

STAFF *lay knife and fork on the table for her.*

EDNA.   Fish! Fish!

She sweeps the cutlery onto the floor.

This behaviour astonishes those around.

A plate containing a kipper is brought her. She sits looking at the kipper. Then seizes it and thrusts it into her mouth, gobbling it up in one bite.

Then she spits it out.

EDNA.   This is poison! Poison! This isn't food! This is snot from your noses! From out your noses!

STAFF.   This is fish sent up specially from the diet kitchen. It's fish—flat fish.

EDNA.   It's snot.

She stuffs the remains of the fish into her mug, cramming it down. Then she starts flipping bits of the fish at OTHER INMATES.

EDNA.   Whee! Whee!

An INMATE *is watching with amusement laughing steadily.*

EDNA *gets up very deliberately and pours the remains of the mug (tea and kipper) over her.*

EDNA *is approached by a thirty-five year old* WOMAN.

51

CLARA. Got any pills?

EDNA. Eh?

CLARA. Got any pills? You don't eat all the pills the
nurses gives you, do you? You puts them under
your tongue and you spits them out don't you?

EDNA. Well, I got a few, but I want them for myself.

CLARA. Go on.

EDNA. Why?

CLARA. Go on—give us some—

EDNA, *after a pause, hands over some pills
from her pocket.*

EDNA. How d'you know that this sort will agree with
you? What's your name, dear?

CLARA. None of your business.

EDNA. Why do you want them pills so bad?

CLARA. Oh, everyone wants pills, dear.

EDNA *follows the* WOMAN *with her eyes,
surprised, as she continues round the room, in
search of more pills.*

EDNA *being given anti-depressant pills. She clamps
her mouth tight shut, but the pills are shoved in by
the* STAFF.

EDNA *removes them, puts them in her pocket.*

EDNA. You're lost. You're all lost . . . Oh all right,
you have my permission, you can go in now.

Solarium

Chairs along the walls on which EDNA, CATRINA *and*
TWO OTHERS *sit.*

52

EDNA.   Well, what's a beautiful girl like you doing here? You're too good-looking to be in here, ducks.

CATRINA.   Them that's the most young and beautiful can be the sickest in their mind, my love.

EDNA.   You sick in your mind, dear? Oh, tut, tut.

CATRINA.   It was them pills, what the doctor give me. Me nerves they got to be terrible. I needed more and more pills to quiet them down. Till I was taking sixty or eighty a day.

EDNA.   Well, I hope your stay here isn't a long one.

CATRINA.   I hope it will be a very, very long one.

She sighs, shrugs, hunches her shoulders, lights a cigarette.

CATRINA *is an exceptionally beautiful, lanky girl of seventeen.*

VOICE *calls.*   Next!

EDNA.   It's the next.

EDNA *goes up to the door.*

Psychiatrist's Office

PSYCHIATRIST.   Ah. Ah. It's Edna, is it? Good. Now can you please try—can you please tell me, if you know it, the date?

EDNA.   The date? Oh, the date—ah—

She thinks for some while, then;

EDNA.   The thirty-second.

PSYCHIATRIST I.   Hmmmm. All right. You can stay in another week.

53

Solarium

PADRE (PATIENT). *to Edna.* I don't believe in titles. But you may as well use mine when you're addressing me. Yes, if it's all right by you, call me Padre.

Outside

A MAN *drilling imaginary trooper, in German, through a megaphone.*

Ward

Silence

STAFF *takes* EDNA, *injects her with a sedative.*

She clamps electrodes on her forehead, helped by an ASSISTANT. *Then puts an electric current through them.*

At the Porter's Lodge

EDNA *is trying to establish contact.*

EDNA.   It gives me hydrophobia. All I could hear is creaking bones. Whose? Whose bones? My bones. Listen.

She cracks bones

EDNA.   I can wrench bones. One against the other. I do it in the ward till they goes mad.

Telephone rings

PORTER *answers it.*

PORTER.   No. Sorry. Sorry. No. I'm sorry she's not
    here.

EDNA.   Hey, did you just have a call for me?

PORTER.   You? Why should I have a call for you, then?

EDNA.   Yes, but I weren't here so you said I weren't here.

PORTER.   I never said you weren't here. It wasn't for
    you.

EDNA.   Yes. I'm sorry. Who was it?

PORTER.   I don't know. A man. But it wasn't for you.

EDNA.   A man! *Why*? Why didn't you let me talk to
    him? I wanted—Iwanted—why didn't you let me
    talk to him?

PORTER.   You are Mrs. Edna Johnson aren't you?

EDNA.   No, Mrs. Edna. . . Oh, forget it.

*With grim intensity, she stumps away from the
lodge.*

The Ward

EDNA.   Where's Clara?—You know, that one went round
    collecting pills.

CATRINA.   Clara? Oh, she's dead. She took too many.

EDNA *thinks this one over for a long time.*

Psychiatrist's Office

PSYCHIATRIST.   You're cured Edna. You still have
    problems, it's true. But basically, yours is not a
    psychological problem. You may have other
    problems, like—housing. As regards your mind

you're as right as rain. And for that reason we can't have you continuing to occupy a bed here which could go to someone who is really sick. You'll have to go Edna.

EDNA. *Hopefully.* I do feel I have some problems.

Kitchen. Night

EDNA *climbs in, turns on gas, stands above stove, reels about.*

Psychiatrist's Office

PSYCHIATRIST. Why did you do it?

EDNA. To show you I wanted to stay.

PSYCHIATRIST. Stay another week. After that go.

EDNA. I'm not staying in this stinking dump.

On the Road

EDNA *is walking.*

EDNA. *sings.* I was never bitter, though my heart was sad,
For many broken friendships litter the road of life
so hard
Blow, savage winds, and bring the slashing rain,
There's a sweetness in her sorrows, and a glory in
her pain

I leave the city, its artificial lights,
Away from the wiles of wanton men and the sensual
delights,
I'll wander along the country, free without a care. . .

In a Barn

EDNA *sits by a fire*

EDNA.   I'll sit by the streams; and breathe deep of
freedom's air!

TWO POLICEMEN *enter. They stamp out the fire.*

The Overgrown back of a Cafe

EDNA *and* IVY *sitting eating beside the dustbins out at
the back of a cafe.*

A MAN *comes out with a fresh dustbin and* EDNA *and*
IVY *get up and begin to peer in it. It contains fruit and
loaves of bread, which they scrabble at.*

The MAN *brings out a bucket of empty tins, potato
peelings, and rubbish off the floor and dumps that on
top.*

EDNA.   Thank you very much.

They continue to scrabble.

On the Road

By the road EDNA, *with an indeterminate bottle, sobs,
drinks Red Biddy.*

EDNA.   I gets drunk very easy. One Red Biddy, and
I'm quickly drunk out of this world.

*A Mercedes-Benz sedan draws up, and leaning from
it,* JAMES, *with a well-educated voice says;*

JAMES.   Er, care for a lift?

EDNA.   Don't you get your hands off me! You keep
your hands on me! Come on! Keep em off me!

JAMES.   No, Honestly, I just asked you if you wanted
a lift?

In the Car

JAMES *is driving.*

EDNA.   The feelings I have about peoples, I'll tell you
the real peoples in life, that they are not like I think
they are or should be, peoples as treat people as
they should treat them which they don't.

JAMES.   I see.

EDNA.   Yes.

JAMES.   *Rather confused.* I see, you feel that?

EDNA.   Why yes, that's so. These people have the run
of experience. All sorts of peoples—oh yes,
absolutely. So that's what I'll say about the
peoples.

   JAMES *thinks ponderously about this piece of
non-information.*

JAMES.   Yes. . . Look, if you're down and out,
St. Gertrude's will give you a bed!

EDNA.   Well, let me tell you now, let me tell you. I'll
tell you now, indeed I am down, very much down
and indeed I'm out, I am right down as you say, in
the gutter and out as a matter of fact, and although
you are a gentleman, I see you're a gentleman no two
ways about it, easy to see, some Lord or other or
businessman, I'm down as a matter of fact, down
in the gutter. . .

   *She has forgotten what she's saying. Then she
remembers, triumphant;*

EDNA.   They won't let you in without money!

JAMES.   Oh, that's nonsense.

EDNA.   Nonsense? Nonsense? No, it's not nonsense. I
went in at St. Gertrude's, I said. . .

Lodging House

A telephone rings.

Behind lodging house, PROPRIETOR II, A MAN

EDNA.   Hey, is that for me?

> *She rushes in the direction of the phone.*

> *The lodging house* PROPRIETOR *wrestles
> with her to prevent her.*

Ruins in Country

A strong wind.

EDNA *wrapping newspapers, old polythene sacks,
etc. round her.*

A TRAMP, *as before, offers* EDNA *a bottle.*

After a pause EDNA *drinks with considerable distaste.*

The Street of a Big Town

EDNA *passes.*

*In her hand she holds a black polythene bag. The pork-
pie hat is stuffed down over her head and her skirts are
so long that they almost rub the ground leaving little
room to see beneath them her grubby stockings.*

*She is trailing along the street being constantly overtaken
by those who walk faster than her.*

At one point she is confused. She has to make a lengthy detour round some building operations blocking the way to the outside snack bar that she often uses.

Then she continues along the dusty streets.

Toilet

A notice says:

'The consumption of alcohol and drug taking in public conveniences have led to serious acts of misconduct. The convenience attendant will call the police immediately any breach of the Corporation's bylaws occur'

Another notice says:

'Loitering is prohibited. Beware of pickpockets.'

EDNA *is scrubbing away at her hands now, trying to get them clean at the rinsing basin of the public toilets.*

Another notice:

'V.D. is nearly always caught by having sex with an infected person.'

At the Charitable Institution

In the clothing store.

ROGO *and* EDNA *are surrounded by long lines of coats and piles of other clothes.*

One side of the room is entirely taken up with piles of boots and shoes.

ROGO *is a kindly man, forty years of age, a down-at-heel peer with a small private income and too little to do.*

ROGO. Only a pound or two, but it comes with the sincere good wishes of everyone concerned with this charity.

He hands her two pounds.

ROGO. Now, what about clothing?

EDNA. The boot, sir? How about the boot sir? I could use a boot, sir.

She holds up her foot.

EDNA. I do a certain amount of strolling around sir. Wear through them quick.

ROGO. Yes. I see. Very good. Yes, we can fit you up with boots.

EDNA *looks through the boots and chooses a stout pair.*

ROGO. Did something happen to you in the past? Was there some sad instance?

EDNA. And a coat?

She demonstrates her threadbare coat.

ROGO. Yes, I think we can help you out in that department. Oh, yes, that one seems very satisfactory. It's almost a perfect fit! Would you like to give me your old coat now?

EDNA. No!

ROGO. Oh!

EDNA. No! 'Never throw away old clothes!'

ROGO. Very sensible!

EDNA *begins to wrap up her old coat with her other things in the polythene.*

ROGO. Then, here's the address of a room that we've

found for you.

EDNA.   I'll find me own place.

She stumps out.

Street

EDNA *trudging doggedly towards us.*

Boarding House

EDNA.   I need a rent book, see, they say.

LANDLADY.   Who's they?

EDNA.   Well like, me employment.

LANDLADY.   Not on the Social Security are you by any chance, dear?

EDNA.   Oh no oh no. I'm in good employment.

LANDLADY.   What sort?

EDNA.   Well, in the passages.

LANDLADY.   Hmm. . .

EDNA.   Oh get away with your hmm. I'm going to the toilet.

The LANDLADY *watches with horror.* EDNA *stumps off towards the toilet at the end of the entrance hall.*

Then she returns abruptly.

EDNA.   Oh no, I'm not staying here. Well, you wouldn't have me anyway, would you?

LANDLADY.   Well, I—uh. . .

EDNA *clutches her stomach.*

EDNA. I got hyderophilia.

She staggers out.

A Common Lodging House

At the bed-ticket window.

EDNA *and a small queue of threadbare* WOMEN *are filing past.*

ATTENDANT (female). Hey you!

EDNA. Eh?

ATTENDANT. What number were you last night?

EDNA. Well, number thirty-four.

ATTENDANT. No, you're sixty-two. You wet your bed, didn't you?

EDNA. I-

ATTENDANT *looks accusingly at* EDNA.

ATTENDANT. Out!

EDNA. Let's have another try!

ATTENDANT. Out!

Social Security Office

A fairly friendly young GIRL CLERK

CLERK. Can you give me your name and permanent address?

EDNA. Eh?

CLERK. Can you give me your name and your permanent—

EDNA. Ain't got no permanent name—

CLERK. Sorry?

EDNA. Ain't got no permanent name, it varies. I mean, sorry, ain't got no permanent address. The name's McLean.

CLERK. Well, I'm sorry, Mrs. McLean; till you've got a permanent address, there's nothing can be done.

EDNA. Yeah, well, something bloody well must be done. I ain't got no money.

CLERK. Sorry, madam, you've got to have a fixed address before one of our inspectors can call in to see you.

She speaks aside to another CLERK *who has heard what is going on.*

CLERK. I could give you a chit to Wolverhampton Buildings.

EDNA. I went there on a chit didn't I? They threw me out!

There are more muttered asides. Then CLERK I *leans across;*

CLERK I. Go to Stockville Department of Health and Social Security, that's in Broad Street, during office hours; or in the hours of darkness to the police station at Digbell. On furnishing proof of destitution they will give you a chit entitling you to claim a bed in the local Part III accommodation.

EDNA *thoughfully attempts to absorb this information.*

A Social Security Office

EDNA *rummages in her parcel.*

EDNA.   Here's me address. And here's me permanent name.

> CLERK *looks at the insurance card that* EDNA *produces.*

CLERK II.   Mr. Robert Tute.

EDNA.   *in a peculiar low voice*   Ah yes. That is my name.

CLERK II.   Are you sure that's your name, er, Mr. Tute?

> EDNA *leaves the office at a fast stoop.*

In a Magistrate's Court

POLICEMAN.   The accused was shouting, striding backwards and forwards, and causing a considerable amount of annoyance. Complaints had been received from neighbours. I informed her that, in my opinion her behaviour was drunk and disorderly and that she was causing a breach of the peace.

Magistrate's Court (II)

SOLICITOR FOR THE PROSECUTION.   Evidence of the second constable is in effect the same as that of the first. Is there any need . . .

MAGISTRATE.   No need. No no no, no need. What have you got to say?

EDNA.   Well, I'm very sorry sir. I didn't seem to do it and I don't know what come over me, that I didn't do it. All I says is, that I didn't seem as how I was doing it. Oh no. Not at all. The fact is, I drank the liquid intending just to have a drop, and, well, I drank a bit more than a drop, didn't I? But I've got me pound saved up. I've got me pound saved up to pay me fine.

MAGISTRATE.   Anything known?

CLERK, A WOMAN .   Yes, in 1917 . . .

MAGISTRATE.   Just the last three.

CLERK.   Two convictions of six months each for drunk and disorderly, two years for larceny.

There is a pause. Then the MAGISTRATE *says;*

MAGISTRATE.   I'm afraid we're going to need more than a one pound fine . . .

The Nick

A cell.

We hear the VOICE *of an* OFFICIAL;

OFFICIAL.   Sir Alexander Paterson, the founder of the idea of Preventive Detention, was well aware that some people are incorrigible and believed that society should be given maximum protection from such people.

In her Cell

The VOICE *of*

EDNA.   It's a quite nice in here ent it? Quite nice doings. I'll say it's a nice place. Well it's warm. It's warmer nor outside I always say prison is not so

67

bad as it's cracked up to be. 'Tis better than some hotels.

Then she looks out a long time through the window.

An Office in the Nick

It is a large room with painted brick walls with one table at which JOSIE *and* EDNA *sit.*

JOSIE.   Of course, if you come to Jesus Saves, we can't have you getting drunk.

EDNA.   I'm not going to take a drink.

JOSIE.   Really, really, oh, well that's very good, Edna.

EDNA.   No, and I will be hanging onto me money, won't be spending all over the place.

JOSIE.   Very good. Very good indeed. Excellent.

EDNA.   I shall be getting up in the morning all right.

JOSIE.   Very good. Excellent.

EDNA.   And I shall be taking the bath two or three times a day.

JOSIE.   Oh well, er, I'd have thought it was enough—two or three times in the *week.* Of course life at Jesus Saves may not be quite like you think it will be.

EDNA.   I am changed. I won't have no trouble at all. I'll behave meself. No matter what people say. I'm changed. No more. No more we'll have no funny ways.

JOSIE.   You'll not only have to get up in the morning. You'll have to go to work.

EDNA.   Guv, that's no trouble in me, I don't care. I've

been a good worker in the past.

JOSIE. Look, the other thing is that if you go out on Friday nights and get yourself drunk—

EDNA. Look, guv, I never drink.

JOSIE. *With a smile.* Hm. Well I begin to wonder what such a virtuous person is doing inside a prison at all unless they happened to be the Governor or the Chaplain?

EDNA. Thank you very much, sir.

JOSIE. Is there not anything else you'd like to tell me about yourself like, about your parents or your background?

There is a pause. Then EDNA *says;*

EDNA. Thank you, sir.

Outside the Nick

EDNA, *complete with her polythene bag, is leaving the nick. We hear her* VOICE;

EDNA. Oh, why didn't they let me stay in the nick, in the nick.

In a Crowded Street

Crossing the street, EDNA *imprudently collides with a motor.*

She lies at the side of the road.

*Night. Under some Arches under a
Railway*

This is a vision of despair. So far we have seen DOSSERS
and DOWN *and* OUTS *in fairly small numbers, and
mainly* WOMEN. *Now we see one of the great gathering
places of* MEN.

We see this first from inside a van driven by NUNS.

There are many RAGGED MEN, *many drunk, many
desperate, running after the van to be first for the soup.*

*They crowd behind the van in a semi-circle, like animals
waiting to be fed.*

The back of the van is opened and the NUNS *in their
flowing garments stagger out carrying between them a
large tureen of soup and cut loaves. They begin to ladle
out the soup into disposable cups. They are helped by*
GRAHAM, *a hippy type charity worker. Other* NUNS

71

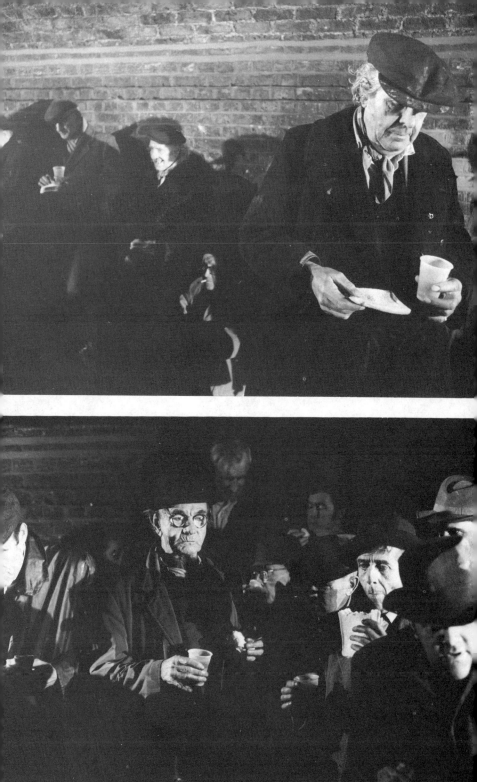

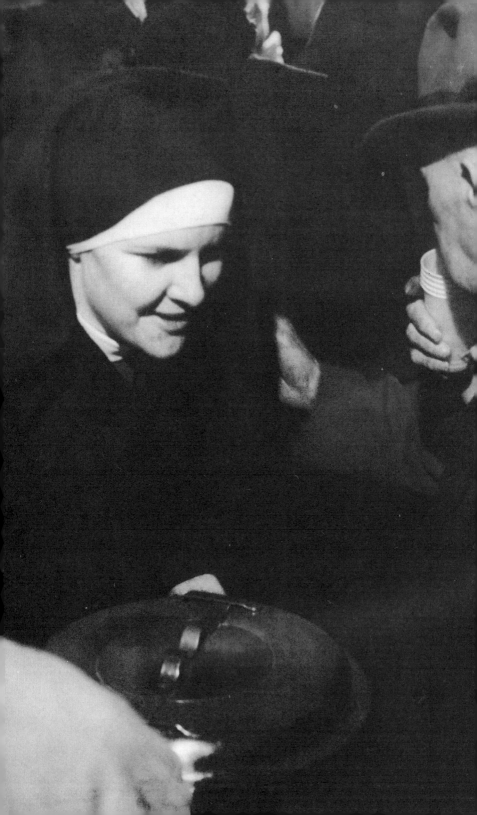

*go round handing out wads of four or five slices of
bread by hand.*

Many of the MEN *have bloated unhealthy complexions.
All wear overcoats. The dust rises in the light from the
headlamps and beneath this arch some of the* MEN *sit
down in the mud with their backs against the walls to
drink their soup and gnaw sometimes with gap-toothed
gums at the large wads of five or six slices.*

When the NUNS, *pretty young girls that they are, give
out the soup or bread they don't at once withdraw
their hand, but leave it a moment, as if offering
spiritual salvation as well as material.*

Only ONE MAN *is annoyed and upset when he is
approached.*

MAN. I don't need your bloody charity. I'll admit I'm
    down, but I'm not out yet. I don't need your
    charity—yet.

NUN. I'm sorry, I didn't mean to offend you.

MAN. No, you're right, I'm down. But not out.

NUN. I didn't mean to offend you.

    ONE MAN *has the trembles and he spills not one
    but three cups of soup before he is able to drink
    it, the soup splashing all over him as if he's been
    sick. He spills it too all over the habit of a pretty
    young* NUN.

    *The soup tureen has now been put back in the van.
    It moves off with back doors open. But* ONE
    DRUNK *with a great blubber lower lip sticking
    out, staggers up to the van, preventing the* NUN
    closing the doors.

DRUNK. Soup, soup, I've only just come.

NUN *in middle of van.* But he's had five soups already.

76

MOTHER SUPERIOR.   Never mind. Quick, quick, give him the soup.

And now the great face of the MAN *is practically in the van and he is swearing 'Fuck! Fuck!'*

MOTHER SUPERIOR.   Quick, by the Mother of God, give him the soup!

But not quick enough.

The MAN *has got half into the van.*

NUN II *gives him soup.*

The MOTHER SUPERIOR *drives on.*

JAMES.   We've given out too much soup. We'll be running short later.

A Large and Luxurious Hotel
Embankment Entrance

DOORMAN *opens car door for sveldt blonde* GIRL. *And now we see a* MAN *sleeping stretched out on a park bench.*

We see a pool of urine beneath bench.

We see OTHER PEOPLE *bedded down for the night on seats of the Embankment Gardens.*

The most sinister of all these in appearance wears a dark suit, and each extremity, hands, feet, head, is completely swathed in newspaper.

Near Staff Entrance of the
Grand Palace Hotel

A street by the Grand Palace Hotel, is the most macabre

*place that they visit. Here there are two big windows
meshed across with wire netting and against this there
cling twenty gaunt silhouettes, clinging on with grubby
fingers, the forgotten people of an age, trying to pick up
a touch of the heat that comes through the grating.*

There is a very tall MAN *with high mongoloid features
standing in the centre of one of the windows.*

Embankment. Night

EDNA *sits on one of the benches, amid the sleeping
figures.*

EDNA.   Feel it! Feel it! They run me down! They run
me down! The bastards!

> *She appears to sink into a deep sleep.
> Then suddenly she wakes up again with a violent
> start as she sees a* NUN *standing before her.*

EDNA.   Oh! I'm Irish! I'm a Catholic! I've sinned.

> *She hides her head in her hands and weeps,
> striking her brow as if at the memory of terrible
> sins. She looks up.*

EDNA.   Here's money for you, here's money for you.

> *She fumbles in her clothes*

A NUN.   We don't want your money. Have you been
to the hospital?

EDNA.   Yes. But they wouldn't have me. They dressed
me knee but that's all they do. Then they threw
me out again. Feel it. Feel my knee!

> A NUN *feels it and it is far larger and far hotter
> than the other.*

NUN.   Have you anywhere to go tonight?

78

EDNA.   No, I've nowhere to go. There's nowhere for
me. Nowhere they'll have me. I'm a Catholic! I'm
Irish! Oh I've sinned.

The NUN *addresses a* MAN *half asleep on the bench
beside her.*

NUN.   Will you be looking after her?

MAN.   Yes, I'll look after her.

NUN.   Here's money for *you.*

Outside Jesus Saves

Hostel. It is a typical house in a typical street. Night.

EDNA *begins at first slowly then faster to skip, up and
down. This time she's really drunk. And, determined
not to be let into Jesus Saves the easy way, she begins
a declamatory aria;*

EDNA.   Call yourselves Christians! Call yourselves
bloody Christians! Call yourselves Jesus Saves, and
you turn me into the bloody night! You've got a
nerve. Jesus Saves indeed. Aw fawk. Jesus saves!
Call yourselves Christians and yet you leave me out
in the night! Aw, fawk off! I hate you!

EDNA *strides angrily up and down the street.*

PEOPLE *shout down from above;*

MAN.   Aw shut up! Fawk off! Learn some behaviour.

EDNA.   All Fawk.

*She is shouting and bawling, hammering on the wrong
door.*

WOMAN.   Shut up! Shut up! Or I'll ring the police.

EDNA.   Fawk! Fawk off!

MAN. Shut up, you bloody vagrant!

There is a menacing pause. Then;

EDNA. Vagrant? Vagrant? I am no vagrant!

MAN. Vagrant? Well if you're not a vagrant I'll call
you mobile. Shut up you bloody mobile.

EDNA. *Shouts.* I'm not a mobile, neither.

MAN. I've got a wife and kids in here. Please shut up!

EDNA *as much to herself as to anyone else;*

EDNA. I don't like the attitude. It is not necessary to
introduce me as a vagrant. I have lived in houses and
have every right to live in houses. Only they always
get pulled down! That's all. That's all the trouble.
I have lived in no less than three houses that have
been condemned and *pulled down* over my head.
Can I help that? I do not like living like I do. I do
not like sharing dormitories. It hurts my feelings
very much when you call me vagrant or a mobile.
A mobile goes on wheels. I am *not* mobile. I do not
go on wheels.

MAN. All I was saying was—

EDNA. It is true I haven't got very much luggage. I
have no nightdress now, I gave it to charity, I have
had no use for nightdress this last six months. I
sent my last one away to Victoria Docks for
charity. But if I have no nightdress this minute
doesn't mean that I don't change my clothes or
wash them or both very frequent. I have always
been to public baths regular, but this doesn't
mean that I am mobile.

MAN. I see. Well now, for Christ sake—

EDNA. Well, *do* you see? Mobile is a mobile car or a
mobile *van.* I am not a car *or* a van. The nightdress

is sold cheaply and contributes to church funds, but you put them *off*! Oh fuck off! Fuck off the lot of you! All fuck!

A light goes on in Jesus Saves, and, like an angel, JOSIE appears in her nightdress.

JOSIE. So Edna! You want to come in?

EDNA. Yes.

JOSIE. Come on.

Meekly, EDNA *follows her into the hostel.*

*Inside Bedroom No. 4 at
Jesus Saves.*

The room is filled with beds in which lie TERESA, VANGI, TRUDI, LIL, SARAH.

EDNA *lies on a mattress, boots and hat and all. She mutters and curses to herself, but mainly happy noises. She swigs from a bottle. She laughs.*

EDNA. Whee!

Some of the OTHER FIGURES *stir.*

EDNA. Whee! Whee!

*Then she sings; 'Knees up Mother Brown!
Knees up Mother Brown!'*

TRUDI. Aw, shut up. Belt up your bleeding row! Belt up with your bleeding row!

EDNA*'s boot gets caught in the mattress and tears it. Then, trying to extricate herself, she gets herself entangled in the blanket, tears that, till she is tied in knots, caught half under the bedding. She shouts;*

EDNA.   I'm being tied up! I fear! Let me go! Keep
these things off me. Oh, I'm being a-tied up! Let
me go! I am a piece of machinery, I was wrongly
connected, leave me be, leave me be. . .

VANGI.   You're not a bit of machinery, darling.

TRUDI *sits up, semi-naked.*

LIL *drinks V.P. wine.*

*The matress rips more, the blanket is knotted in
shreds around her, she tears the blanket, feathers
emerge from the pillows. An amazing amount of
confusion is caused by the* OLD LADY.

EDNA.   Oh me asthma! Oh, me asthma!

TRUDI *tries to help her.*

EDNA *objects to the attentions of this naked
girl.*

There is a free for all, in the midst of which
JOSIE *comes in again and speaks to her,
severely;*

JOSIE.   Edna! Shut up! Shut up! Go back to bed!

EDNA *surprisingly subsides.*

EDNA.   All right.

*She takes off garments; a man's sports jacket, her
greatcoat, shirt, vest, another shirt, still leaving her
in combinations. She puts her greatcoat back on,
settles down on the remains of the mattress, and
goes to sleep.*

Bedroom No. 4. Next Morning

*They are dressing. Meanwhile we hear the endless
droning* VOICE *of* TERESA, *talking to* EDNA.

TERESA.   I didn't think nothing of it. I thought that's
how it always was. But as I got older, I got so I
didn't like so much of it. That was after me real
Mum died. And one day when I was twelve when
me new Mum, that's me step-Mum, was going out
shopping I said, 'Please take me too, Mum, 'cos I
don't like my Dad taking me to bed with him when
you go out. So then it all came out. My step-Mum sent
for the police and the policewoman she come along
and she said; 'You said you have had intercourse with
him?' And I said; 'I don't know. What's intercourse?'
And she said 'You must know what intercourse is,
girl.' So I said 'No.' So she said, 'Well, did he get his
thing out and put it up you?' and I thought she
meant his tongue because he had been kissing me.

In the Kitchen at Jesus Saves

As the INMATES *prepare breakfast,* TERESA's *story
drones on and on;*

TERESA.   So I said, yes. And they took us to the Court,
and then in the Court my Dad got a priest to stand
by and say that my Dad would never do a thing like
that and then they got a doctor to examine me and
he said that I was not a virgin. So then they said if
it wasn't my Dad it must be someone else and I was
in need of moral protection. And there was no place
in the Children's Home. So I went to a Remand Home
and that's about it I suppose. I felt my Dad didn't
want me really. And it upset me when they didn't
trust my word and I didn't think things should be
like that between a Dad and his daughter.

In the Washroom

The monologue continues in the washroom.

TERESA. I had a little baby later and I loved her but they took her from me.

> EDNA, *trying to get away from this endless story turns to* LIL;

EDNA. Hey, int I seen you before somewhere?

> *Meanwhile* TRUDI, *an attractive girl, but with pockmarked face, confronts* EDNA;

TRUDI. That one over there, that's Mavis. She drowned her daughter, aged two, the day after she was refused abortion for a second child she was expecting . Who else is there? Oh, there's Rosamund. There was a new-born baby girl found strangled and wrapped in a brown paper parcel in the women's public lavatories. Know whose it was?

> *Later,* LEONA, *a very beautiful girl, corners* EDNA; *she's half cockney, half Indian.*

LEONA. At the Children's Home I've seen strange sights in the woods.

EDNA. What sort of sights?

LEONA. Oh I don't know. You imagine strange things and you come back and tell the other children, which are lies. When they talk about happy homes we got to wonder how, why, why not me? I've seen strange sights in the woods, banshees and ghosts. They come back and *want* you.

> LEONA *gazes with wide eyes.*

In the Kitchen

EDNA *sits down to a breakfast of baked beans.*

84

In the 'garden' of Jesus Saves

TERESA *and* EDNA *are hanging sheets.*

TERESA. I met a fella and I thought it was sex and
excitement I was after but now I see it was only
affection. I met another man. His name was Jimmy.
But I couldn't get pregnant again although I'd had
a child by the first man. Then at last I did become
pregnant and not so long after that I started
bleeding. But the next day when I was in bed I
heard my first kid screaming. I jumped out of bed
and saw my husband attacking the baby with a fork.
And when I was stopping him the bleeding started
again and I had a miscarriage. I took the kid with
me because I didn't think it was safe to leave him
there. But Jim went one afternoon and took him
away. So then I went down to Eastbourne and lived
with my Mum. I took too many aspirins and the
police took me to the Institution.

In the Dormitory

EDNA *climbs in one of the beds in the dormitory.*

*She hunches herself up in the foetus position in one
corner.*

JOSIE *comes in suddenly.*

EDNA *sits up horrified, scared out of her wits, staring
ahead, a terrified old lady.*

JOSIE. I startled you, Edna!

EDNA *goes to sleep again.*

On another occasion we see EDNA *asleep.*
Then she sits up and shouts;

EDNA. She's been a piece of machinery! Now she's

wrongly connected.

On another occasion we again see EDNA *in bed, and she's drunk.*

EDNA.   Whee! Whee!

TRUDI, *naked, straddles the bed where* EDNA *sleeps, she opens her bare legs wide.*

TRUDI.   Look at this, Edna!

EDNA *wakes up and howls in disgust.*

The Office at Jesus Saves

A Committee Meeting is in progress, GRAHAM, SUE *(Graham's girlfriend),* JOSIE, *the* MOTHER SUPERIOR.

Suddenly TRUDI *staggers in. She throws a fit.*

TRUDI.   Go on, kill me! Kill me!

TRUDI *is forcibly expelled by* GRAHAM *and* JOSIE.

MOTHER SUPERIOR.   We really ought to throw her out.

JOSIE.   No one else will take her. Even the Psychiatric Hospital. I phoned them again last week. They said 'We can't take her. She's absolutely mad.'

MOTHER SUPERIOR.   According to our constitution, they're only meant to stay two weeks.

VICTOR, *ineffectual but kind.*   Yes. But after this, it really is the gutter. We can't turn them out.

The telephone rings. JOSIE *answers it.*

JOSIE.   Yes? Yes. Oh yes. Yes. I see. Yes. Yes. Yes, can do.

The OTHERS *continue to speak quietly as*
JOSIE *talks.*

MOTHER SUPERIOR. She hangs on to you. She drains
you. She just won't leave you. She's been out in
the street, exposes herself.

VICTOR. Yes, she even said to me, 'Are you taking me
out?' That turned me off.

JOSIE *finishes her phone call.*

JOSIE. Yes, yes. Yes, can do.

She puts down the phone.

GRAHAM. She seems to get guys though.

SUE. But where does she take them to?

GRAHAM. Oh, just on the back seat of their cars.

SUE. She can't really be attractive to men though.

VICTOR. She's young. That's enough.

A bumping sound has been intermittently heard.

VICTOR. By the way, what is that bumping sound?

SUE. I think it's Edna cleaning up.

They all smile.

JOSIE. Anyway, Trudi; I do tell her she has to go but
when I do this she immediately indulges in a fit of
screaming. The other day she told me 'I'm going to
keep an exact record of all my fits. Then I shall ring
and tell the press.' I said, 'They wouldn't be
interested.' She said 'Well they should be.'

VICTOR. Yes, and indeed, I suppose that they should
be. Really.

MOTHER SUPERIOR. It's not as if these were the only
ones. I believe that every day now you're having to

turn people away?

JOSIE.   I do, I do. All the time women and girls are coming to the door, asking to be taken in. Every day I have to turn four or five away.

MOTHER SUPERIOR.   Why do we discriminate in favour of the ones we've got, against the others?

The Hall

EDNA *sweeping.*

VANGI *comes into the house with shining eyes.*

VANGI.   Hullo everybody! I've just been up the town centre, everybody's there, it's crazy, everyone in England almost, they're just all stoned, just lying around. I don't know what's happening to this country. I think everybody's going to be over-whelmed. They've put stuff in the reservoirs. Then the Japs'll come!

In the Kitchen

EDNA.   What is all this meat? It's nearly all bone!

JOSIE.   We live on what we're given.

They are sorting out red meat from a cardboard box, and mounds of garments and other food which has been left for them.

JOSIE.   There was a time when we had only veal and ham pies—two foot long, thirty of them. For weeks we ate veal and ham pies until we had veal and ham sticking out of our ears. Then another time a super-market dumped three hundred eggs on us. They were all on the point of going off.

LIL. Yes. I remember the time!

JOSIE. So many omelettes! We have a very good
arrangement with the butcher now. Any bits of
meat that fall on the floor, or something like that,
he gives them us. My idea was of a self-supporting
society in which this house slowly grew into a
street owned by us and then a town, then into
greater and greater units. The barriers that are set
up by the usual form of social worker, that is, a
desk, is completely wrong, and I felt that one can
draw an analogy with someone down a well in which
the usual form of approach is to drop down a rope
and say, Hang on to this and we'll pull you up, but
I took the attitude that one should get down into
the well and help push from alongside you.

Something of this has got through to EDNA *who turn
turns and says excitedly to* JOSIE;

EDNA. This place is a palace. I've tried all the others.
Well this is a nice place. A very very very nice place.

JOSIE. Well, thank you!

The OTHERS *laugh pleasurably and shyly.*

Bedroom 4. Night

JOSIE *sits on a bed listening, indulgently, as* EDNA
undresses.

EDNA. A lot of them hostels, it's like in a tank, like the
fish, close the doors, and hope for the best. But
that's not the best way to treat them sort of people.

The OTHERS *are undressing, some of them are by
now asleep.*

EDNA. I'm prepared to work. Oh yes. But when I go

89

they say—'How old are you?' And I say, 'How old?'
They say; 'Are you a good timekeeper?' And I say;
'Yes. Yes and in good 'ealth.' So she says; 'Can you
work without supervision?' Yes. And I think, this
is getting interesting. But then, it often happens,
they sort of . . . look me over and then . . . sort of
flitters out. It's not that they isn't genuine. Just
I suppose, them persons don't have a very good
memory.

JOSIE. Now, can you begin to settle down and go to
sleep? You can't talk all the night.

EDNA. I have to. My doctor says I must be able to
talk. Most important. Talk all the time.

JOSIE. *Indulgently.* Even so. You must go to sleep
now.

She goes out.

EDNA *closes her eyes.*

For a second time, TRUDI *opens her legs wide
just above where* EDNA *is lying.*

TRUDI. Look at this, Edna!

EDNA. Oh—no—damn you!

In the Office

TRUDI. You don't want me to stay do you? Admit it,
you *want* me to leave. You don't want me here.
All right, I'll go.

A pause.

JOSIE. *Delighted, but trying not to show it*   All right
then, Trudi, go.

A long pause.

We notice at the back of the room, LIL *is drinking Brasso.*

From behind her back TRUDI *brings a parcel.*

TRUDI.   They're roses for you, Josie. Roses!

TRUDI *embraces* JOSIE.

Outside Jesus Saves. Late into
the Night

EDNA.   Fawk! All fawk!

she bangs at door.

EDNA.   Let me in! Fawk! Fawk! All fawk! Let me in!

She bangs at the door, then tilting for a moment beside the window, she takes aim and smashes it.   .

In the Office. Late the same Night

EDNA *has sobered up.*

EDNA *and* JOSIE *chewing gum.*

EDNA.   I thought you was going to throw me out.

JOSIE.   Oh no, Edna, we wouldn't do that.

EDNA.   Will I be with you for always?

JOSIE.   Well no, not for always—but . . .

EDNA.   Is there any like me in the world? I mean, many like me?

JOSIE.   What, people that tramp.

EDNA.   Well, you know, the no-good ones.

JOSIE.   I don't think you're no good.

91

EDNA.   What they call the inadequate ones.

JOSIE.   Yes, but inadequate for what? Does that mean just inadequate to cope with a society that is itself inadequate?

JOSIE *chews on some chewing gum.*

EDNA.   You hate that stuff, don't you.

JOSIE.   Oh no. Oh no. I don't hate it.

EDNA.   Yes you do. You hate it. Why do you always chew this bloody chewing gum when I give it you although you hate it?

JOSIE.   Edna, I'll admit I don't really like it.

EDNA.   But you chew it.

JOSIE.   I chew it for the sake of our friendship.

EDNA.   Our friendship! Our friendship! Whee! Whee! Oh well!

JOSIE.   Even if at the end you're going to touch me for fifty p.

EDNA.   Ha! Our friendship! Well, Josie, you, well, have you got a dollar to lend me?

JOSIE *not sure how to answer this.*

EDNA.   Somebody told me how God is dead.

JOSIE.   Oh yes. I'm sure. Not dead, but insane. This world is not the creation of a sane person.

EDNA.   Am *I* sane?

JOSIE.   Who knows. Tell me, when you first came to the hostel, why didn't you come the ordinary way—without causing all that disturbance?

EDNA.   I don't ask no favours of no one.

In the Office

JOSIE, TERESA, EDNA.

EDNA. Well, this fellow keeps phoning, and when I ask
what he wants, he seems to think I want him. What
do you want? he keeps asking. Can I help you?
What do you want? Can I help you?

Bedroom 4

TERESA*'s Lesbian 'boyfriend'.*

'THE MAN' *whispers.* Marry me, Teresa.

TERESA *shouts.* Oh no. No! Shut up! Belt you!
Bugger off!

In the Office

EDNA. I haven't had a drink for three weeks.

JOSIE. Very good, Edna.

EDNA. That's my pride. My pride and my boast.
No drink for three weeks, going out to celebrate!

JOSIE. Oh is that the best . . .

Then she realises that EDNA *has made a joke.*

EDNA *laughs in delight that she's got a rise out
of* JOSIE.

EDNA. April fool!

Room in Town Hall

A public inquiry is in progress.

The CHAIRMAN *sits at one side of a large table.*

To his right and left COUNSEL *representing Local Planning Authority and* COUNSEL *representing Jesus Saves, with* ADVISERS *and* WITNESSES.

The COUNSEL *has a way of wrinkling up the side of his face so that he looks like a gargoyle.*

COUNSEL *for the L.P.A.*   Sir, I represent the interests of the local authority and the inhabitants of Wye Street, who welcome the opportunity of this public enquiry to put forward their point of view. Er, the street is the seat of very considerable amenities of solid respectable people. It was built in, ah, Victorian times as a residential suburb for the business classes and for retired people, and its inhabitants like to think it has retained certain of these excellent characteristics.

Sir, without planning permission, there has been set up in this street a hostel for homeless and inebriate women. The effect on the character of the neighbourhood can only too easily be imagined.

What formerly was a highly respectable neighbour-hood now, it turns out, runs the risk of changing—with grave attendant risks—into something very different.

It was mainly, sir, nuns that did this. They were offered the house, sir, for a few years by a well-wisher. Having no use for it themselves, they lent it to a Miss Josie Quinn for her to carry out in it her experiments with women.

Some of the WOMEN *from the Hostel are among the audience, including* EDNA *and* TRUDI.

COUNSEL.   So, sir, though it is the Mother Superior who carries ultimate responsibility, the everyday decisions are taken by this Josie Quinn.

She is—some sort of idealist. Now why did the nuns who inherited Jesus Saves and its other sponsors, choose this particular street? For this hostel? Did they do this after exhaustive scrutiny of available properties in this or other areas until they found the sort of thing they were looking for? Did they consult maps, the town plan?

No. When we investigate it we find that they are making use of this house and filling it with inebriate women because they were *offered* it.

We see the face of VICTOR *in the audience.*

COUNSEL. They were offered it by a resident of this Borough, and so they never chose this house. No, it was offered them and so they have taken it over, just because—not for any other reason—except that they were offered it. And not knowing what to do with it, they handed it over to this—Miss Quinn—for her experiments.

In the Town Hall. Later

A HOUSEHOLDER *has been called as witness.*

HOUSEHOLDER I. I have been stopped in the street and asked for coppers by both men and women. Their behaviour is drunk and their manner is drunk and sitting on my doorstep and lying on my doorstep is no place for them—drunk.

Later again

HOUSEHOLDER II. A man came in my hall and he asked for water. He followed me into the kitchen when I went to get it and said; 'Have you got any bread?' I refused him and so then he took the

96

water and threw it over me.

HOUSEHOLDER III.   The street is often filled with drunkards. They fall down in the gutter. They're nothing but vagrants.

But hearing this word is too much for EDNA. *Suddenly her voice chirps up from the back of the hall.*

EDNA.   Vagrant! I am not the vagrant!

OTHERS.   Shh!

Later

COUNSEL *for Jesus Saves is cross-examining* HOUSEHOLDER III.

COUNSEL.   You'd agree that this problem should be tackled at its roots?

HOUSE HOLDER III.   I know that these people are ill. But I don't see why they should be accommodated next to people who have been paying their rents and rates for the past thirty years. These people should be somewhere else. In a large hostel, for instance, or a large hotel.

COUNSEL *for the L.A.*   One of our witnesses was unfortunately too sick to attend. Her name is Mrs. Wineberg. So Mrs. Behan will be reading out her statement.

MRS. WINEBERG.   No, here I am!

MRS. WINEBERG *is a very decrepit lady, looking*

rather like the inmates of the hostel.

COUNSEL. *Firmly.* She was too infirm to attend.

MRS. WINEBERG. But she came! She came!

COUNSEL. So Mrs. Behand will be reading out her testimony;

MRS. BEHAN. 'These people are a menace in the street.'

MRS. WINEBERG. She's here! She's here!

MRS. BEHAN. Oh, she's here is she? Oh, then she can read her own testimony.

MRS. WINEBERG *has to be helped to her feet.*

MRS. WINEBERG *reading.* 'These people are a menace to the street. You hear them passing at all hours of the night. When the telly is on we put down the mortice lock. There comes a bang on the door. Who's that? they ask. There's no one here, I say. They are mistaking it . . . '

CHAIRMAN. Mistaking it for what?

MRS. WINEBERG. Heaven knows. For a bus, Or a taxi. Or a train, I suppose. Mistaking it for where they wanted to go.

COUNSEL *for Jesus Saves.* Are the inmates of Jesus Saves in any sense prostitutes?

JOSIE. This is a clean population. The drunken population of these parts is a very clean population. On the whole. They're very clean folk. On the whole. But the need for somewhere for them to go is desperate.

Here are some typical examples of the sort of person we try to help in our hostel.

98

Mary: She's had frequent visits to prison. She needs help desperately.

Trudi: She's not able to work, and permanently confused.

Judith: She's got a police record.

There is shocked comment from HOUSEHOLDERS.

Teresa: She has been in a psychiatric hospital.

Edna: She can be relied on absolutely when she's sober.

And the next woman is permanently confused.

And the next one has had frequent falls.

COUNSEL *for Jesus Saves.* Unless hostels are found for them, you say that many in fact end up in the gutter?

JOSIE. Were it not for this hostel, they would be going to court very frequently at a very great cost to the taxpayer, and going on to prison or psychiatric hospitals at a cost to the taxpayer of many pounds per week.

COUNSEL *for Jesus Saves.* If there is no hostel provided for these people . . .

JOSIE. They have nowhere to go, poor dears, except to the mental hospital or the streets. Or to prison.

NEIGHBOUR. Prison!

JOSIE. Going there, not because they are really criminals or mad but because there's nowhere more suitable for them. These people are referred to in official reports as inebriates, alcoholics, schizophrenics, drug addicts, the disabled, layabouts, failures. These words are alibis to help us to ignore why they're really like they are. Stack the cards

99

against us, these people are the same as us—you and me in a mess.

The answer, so I believe most sincerely, is in the sort of hostel that we have set up. Let us help them. They can exist and be happy in a hostel like ours. They *can* live fulfilled lives. There should be hostels like this everywhere. One every four or five streets.

The places where they're put at present are no answer. The huge institution, so vast, so impersonal. What they need is a small place, a place to be a typical home, the home that most of them never had. They escape the help that is their right because they can't dress up their needs in the correct form. And so they get knocked from pillar to post. And there are thousands of them. I reckon something like one hundred thousand of people littering lunatic asylums, prison, common lodging houses, spikes, sleeping out in the open, mostly men, but a few thousand women.

And the need is desperate. Every day I have to turn women and girls, even men, families away from my door. I don't want to have to turn these away as well. By looking only at their symptoms, society has made an alibi for throwing them away.

COUNSEL. There is nothing to prevent alcoholics banging on the door as word gets around. Is there? Are the doors kept locked?

JOSIE. The doors aren't kept locked, because we want the residents to look on the place as their home.

COUNSEL. Are they let out?

JOSIE. Yes. For purposes of obtaining employment. And of seeing their friends. And for so many other reasons.

COUNSEL. And when they are out—they have a drink?

100

JOSIE. We hope that they will not be slipping back into the state of mind when they want a drink.

COUNSEL. But some *do* relapse . . .?

JOSIE. Very occasionally they relapse.

The angry HOUSEHOLDERS *snarl amongst themselves.*

ANGRY HOUSEHOLDER. Relapse! Want a drink!

COUNSEL. Well then, here we have these inebriate drunken women, staggering back home. A 'staggering ground' for inebriates and alcoholics. A 'gravitation of drunks', I might call it, losing themselves, knock on the wrong door?

JOSIE. Not really. I've heard many complaints against drunks, but never that they knock on the wrong door.

EDNA. Ha ha!

COUNSEL. Sometimes don't they cry out with some persistence, knocking at various doors in the street?

JOSIE. Well, not in my experience. Vagrant alcoholics perhaps. But not these.

EDNA. Vagrant? Vagrant?

HOSTEL INMATES. Shhh!

VICTOR. Most of them have of course come to their present homeless unemployable state through something that's happened in the past. It may be a child has died, and they've never quite got over it. Or that a husband has walked out on one of them, and then of course the question is, why did he walk out? What happened before that—before that sad instance? And so they try to win forgetfulness for a time, either through drink or,

101

more important now, through meths or surgical spirits, or through drugs.

COUNSEL.   How many of these you are housing could be described as vagrants?

EDNA.   Listen, I have said this before. I am not the vagrant! No, I mean it, I am not the vagrant!

CHAIRMAN.   Oh, er—

EDNA.   You think I'm nothing! Nothing! Well I am. Well I'm not. I'll tell you. I've had money and men and I've had women and me own house and I wasn't satisfied. Yes and now I'm a dosser begging for food and I'm still not satisfied. Oh, you're trapped all ways . . . Whee! Whee! Whee! You think I'm nothing don't you? Well, I'm not! I am not. No. Never say that, because I am not.

There is uproar, as people try to restrain EDNA *and* OTHERS *shout. At length* JOSIE *leads* EDNA *out.*

A small Hardware Shop

EDNA.   One large bottle of methylated spirit.

SHOPKEEPER.   Yes. Here you are. That will be thirty-two—

EDNA.   Keep your eff-ing money.

SHOPKEEPER.   Thirty-two p. madam.

EDNA.   Look, before you can even call the shades I can wreck this shop for you.

With her boot she kicks at a pile of tins.

They clatter to the floor.

SHOPKEEPER.   Thirty-two p. madam!

EDNA.   Thirty-two *what?*

She kicks vigorously.

SHOPKEEPER.   All right madam, have it, have it . . .

A Crowded Street or Station
Afternoon rush hour

EDNA *addresses crowds as they surge past. Her tone is now ritualistic;*

EDNA.   Jack off, you runts. . . . Jack it in . . . Devil's pox fall on the top of your crowns. And you bloody old shades, let the worms get at you. When did you ever help, 'stead of punish? When did you help, not harm? Jack off the shades. Jack off the ordinary folk. Jack off the lot. Call yourselves Christians. Call yourselves Christian country. Jack off the lot.

EDNA *rampages around.*

In a Nunnery Chapel. Night

EDNA *, drunk, is climbing a huge cross above the altar.*

A Corridor in the Nunnery. Night

EDNA, *singing, shouting drunkenly, staggering between nuns' cells.*

NUNS *appear and catch her as she shouts and sings. They calm her down.*

NUN.   Hey, isn't this one of the women from the hostel?

EDNA.   Don't turn me out! Don't turn me out!

EDNA *escapes.*

EDNA *shouting, swearing. The* NUNS *persuing her.*

EDNA*'s shouting, screaming face.*

EDNA.   What the effing effing effing . . .

Her shouts become a BABY *screaming.*

EDNA.   Mummy, Mummy, Mummy!

*Now, in a series of almost subliminal flashes
away from her screaming face, we go into flashback.*

*Edna's Mum's Place (Sixty
Years back)*

EDNA's MUM *holds* EDNA *as a* BABY *screaming.*

EDNA's MUM.   I love you Edna. I love you. You're
Mumie's little baby. There then. What do you think
of your daughter?

EDNA's DAD.   It matters eff all to me. I didn't want
her.

Edna's Mum's Place

EDNA *as a little girl looking from a window.*

EDNA.*Voice off, her present age.*   I say as people
sometimes don't look after their peoples. Excepting
the Jews. Jews peoples look after their peoples. And
the coloured peoples.

Edna's Mum's Place

EDNA's MUM *playing with* EDNA.

MUM *is 28, bedraggled, overburdened, a depressed deluded Irish woman.*

MUM. Oh, you're lovely, Edna. You're Mummy's own and lovely little girl. Bless you.

Edna's Mum's Place

EDNA *watches her* MUM *lying on the floor.*

MUM. I'm dead. I'm dead. I'm quite dead now. Here I lie. I'm dead. Where's your Dad, I'm lying in me tomb.

Edna's Mum's Place. Night

The CHILDREN *are sitting round a table.*

MUM. There's no dinner tonight. I'm sorry no dinner tonight, nothing, none.

Edna's Mum's Place. Night

MUM. *Why* you got no money?

DAD. Mmmm. Mmmmmm.

MUM. Cos you drunk it all. That's why. Cos you drunk up all your money. Jesus I'm going to kill you.

EDNA. *Aged 5.* Why are you going to kill Jesus?

Edna's Mum's Place. Night

DAD *beating* MUM *up in the middle of the night.*
Terrified CHILDREN.
Then he's making love to her.

Edna's Mum's Bedroom. Night

DAD *and* MUM *cuddling in bed.*

Edna's Mum's Place

EDNA's DAD *embracing* EDNA.

Edna's Mum's Place

EDNA *(5)*, OTHER KIDS, *and* DAD *dispirited in the background.*

MUM.   You maybe will have to go to a home, kids.

EDNA.   Ent this our home?

MUM.   If you Dad don't make more money you'll have to go to a home.

Edna's Mum's Place. Night

DAD *with a suitcase.*

EDNA.   Don't go out Daddy. Don't go out.

Edna's Mum's Place. Night

DAD.   I went for the job, but they wouldn't have me.

MUM. You're workshy aren't you? You don't want a job do you?

DAD. I do want a job. I do want a job.

MUM. You don't want no job. Your Dad's Jesus. He's bloody Jesus. He's the old martyr type. Caught on the bloody old cross. I'm going to kill him.

Then she sits and stares pathetically into space.

Edna's Mum's Place

EDNA's MUM *with a* SAILOR.

MUM. I'm going out for an hour. I've left your food on the table.

At Mum's Place. Bedroom. Night

CHILDREN *in the filthy room. The* CHILDREN *are crying. Child Care* OFFICER *and* POLICEWOMAN.

OFFICIAL. Where's your Mum?

EDNA. Out at a party.

OFFICIAL. When did you last see her?

EDNA. Last night.

OFFICIAL. I'm going to take you off to a lovely home.

EDNA. But this is home.

Outside Edna's Mum's Place

MUM. Don't you take my children from me! Don't you dare take my children from me! No. No! Don't you take my children from me!

There is a fight and the KIDS *are taken.*

In Court

MAGISTRATE. We must nonetheless accept that you left your children alone all night. I sentence you to three months in prison.

MUM. But that way the poor dears will be alone for ninety nights!

OFFICIAL. May I apply for a custody order for the children to be placed in care of the board of poor law guardians?

MAGISTRATE. Custody order granted.

In the Workhouse

MATRON. Yes, the bed is hard and lumpy, isn't it? That's because you wet it. It's pebbles and marbles. Each time you wet it there will be more. Here is a basin, as you see it is filled with urine. I'm going to wash your face in it. You know why—

EDNA. I wish I could have stayed with my brothers and sisters.

EDNA*'s face plunged into urine.*

EDNA *wears grey coat and hat, black stockings, black shoes.*

The MATRON *has white starched cuffs and a white starched apron.*

Streets. Night

EDNA *and* BOYS. *1925.* EDNA *aged sixteen.*

BOYS.   Come on, Ed, give us a cuddle.

Court

MUM.   She is absolutely uncontrollable. I can't do
anything with her. I've been having to turn boys
away from the door. She'll be better back in the
care of the guardians.

EDNA's DAD *speaks from the dock.*

DAD.   I'm through with you, girl. You've brought
disgrace on us, we've moved into a new district,
the people around are good people, and they don't
know about you. We just don't want you. We don't
want you hanging around.

MAGISTRATE.   Would you care to say anything more
about your daughter?

MUM.   I have no daughter.

In the Nunnery

As EDNA *weeps and rampages around we hear the
voice of;*

EDNA.   Oh Mummy, why did you do that to me?

HOUSEHOLDER II.   Good riddance, good riddance. We
have had to call the police on many occasions to
clear the doorway.

HOUSEHOLDER I.   We have enough trouble already
with drunks, drunken men, fighting and doing
things. The children see it.

The Office

EDNA.   I don't expect you'll want to see me again?

JOSIE *after a pause.*   You expect me to say that don't you Edna. You expect me to be a rejecting father-figure to you. I'm not going to. Just to give you a shock. I'm not going to say; You're a dreadful failure and you've let us down dreadfully. No, Edna. I'm going to say, Well done. You've done a jolly good job Edna in going straight and sober for the length of time you did. Let's see if next time it can't be even longer.

Crowded Street

EDNA *stands, holding a handmade sign; 'Please give generous to Jesus Saves'.*

At her feet is her hat ready to receive any coins offered.

Office

JOSIE   *reads.* 'I am instructed to inform you that the Minister has given every consideration to your petition that Jesus Saves should be legalised and continue to be allowed to operate as a hostel in Wye Street.

JOSIE *continues to read to* INMATES *gathered, including* EDNA.

JOSIE.   'Having taken into account the views of all the relevant parties expressed at the Public Enquiry, he is regretfully forced to reach the conclusion that it is not in the public interest to operate a hostel in this particular area. You have one month from this date to cease operations.'

I'm sorry girls . . .

The Toilet

EDNA.   Oh no, Oh no! Oh Mum, why did you spawn
me? Why did you bring me into the world? Why
did you let me? Why did you ever let me be?

She slashes her wrist across with a rusty knife.

EDNA.   Wasn't there ways? Wasn't there ways of
stopping me ever be?

The Office

TRUDI *shows a wrist-watch.*

JOSIE.   Where did you get that?

TRUDI.   I nicked it. Send for the law to put me back
in the nick.

The telephone rings.

JOSIE. *answers.*   No. I'm sorry. No. No. No. I'm
sorry. No, No, well, the hostel is closing, no we
can't fit you in, I told you we've got to close.

EDNA *appears at the door.*

JOSIE.   Edna, it wasn't for you.

EDNA. *angry.* What's that you say?

JOSIE.   No. Really, Edna. It wasn't for you. Edna,
your wrist!

Outside Jesus Saves. Night

GIRLS *gathered round the door.*

GIRL I. You come from St. Rudolph's Hostel?

JOSIE. Yes?

GIRL I. Well, they're closing.

JOSIE. Good gracious, not another hostel closing tonight?

GIRL I. You got any beds tonight?

JOSIE. Girls, I'm sorry, we're closing.

Behind these TWO GIRLS *in the darkness we see* ANOTHER GIRL *whose face seems familiar. She stands there listening to the* OTHER GIRLS. *Before the* OTHERS *leave she has sunk back into the night.*

Bedroom 4. Night

EDNA *fastening a bandage.*

JOSIE. So, where are you going, Edna?

EDNA. Oh, I'll be all right. Don't worry, I'll move on. After this place I feel so set up I'd quite like to have a bit of time sleeping out.

JOSIE. I hope you'll be all right.

EDNA. I'll be the restless type, see. I was always restless. I couldn't stick anything long.

Kitchen. Night

It is empty.

Dormitory. Night

It is empty. Mattresses rolled up.

Office. Night

Empty.

On the Road. Night.

EDNA *and* TERESA.

EDNA.   Anyway, there was this fella I met long ago,
it was. I did love this fellow, he was the one, as
far as I was concerned. He was my fairy prince.
When I thought of him, when I see the trees
with the clouds in their branches, when I hear in
the papers about, you know, her dreams come true.
Prince Charming, all that, that's when I get to
thinking, thinking about him. He was the only one
really you see. I thought he was my prince
charming, but he was that for some others as well,
other ladies. Anyway, it seems that he didn't
think of me the same way that what I thought
of him sort of. But I still think of him sometimes.
Wondering what it would have been like. Love's
funny, isn't it? I mean, why him?

TERESA.   Did you ever have any children, Edna?

EDNA.   Yes, I had one, but it was a prem. Then I
had another, but that was took away. Well,
cheerio, dear. Cheerio now.

TERESA *would like to be with her.*

TERESA.   Oh, cheerio. Aren't you—Edna—can't we . . .
couldn't we go on together a bit of . . .

EDNA.   Bye bye now, dear. 'Cos I go this way now.
Modern life is so fast and so smart that for them as
is not smart enough . . . well, what I say, flitter
flitter . . .

*She continues to talk and her voice fades away in
the distance as she passes back into the night.*

THE STORY BROUGHT UP TO DATE

The notes that follow were written with the help of Anton Wallich-Clifford, of the Simon Community, and Tom Gifford of the Cyrenians.

CHAR (the Campaign for the Homeless and Rootless), founded since *Edna* was written, was set up to provide 'an officially recognised voice for the various voluntary organisations concerned with care of the single homeless.' It has 130 organisations as members—organisations of all types, ranging from the Church Army to Shelter to the Cyrenians.

Other organisations which have been particularly active in their concern for the single homeless since *Edna* was written are The National Association for Mental Health, the National Association for the Care and Resettlement of Offenders, and the Child Poverty Action Group.

The amount of available accommodation for the single homeless has been increasing. The NACRO handbook in 1961 listed only twelve hostels to which the single home-less could be sent. By 1973 the number listed had risen to over 300, and now stands at over 500.

Workers in the voluntary field have noticed that the level of cooperation by local authorities has become more friendly over the last five years. There seems to be a new attitude on the part of magistrates and judges in giving probation, provided offenders go to a hostel. The attitude of the public has also been improving.

There is now less of the hard drug problem that had reached its height in 1968. Now the treatment centres set up by the government are coping with this particular aspect of single homelessness.

At an international level, care for the single homeless is growing. In Australia, Canada, America, New Zealand, there is a greater realization of the needs of dossers, and British organisations have been helping in this.

But steady improvement in the situation has now come to an end. Since the recession, the work is hampered almost everywhere by shortage of funds.

Local authorities who once made money available for hostels for the single homeless, are now doing so less; as a result some beds in hostels actually stand empty.

Those who are concerned with the single homeless still find themselves battered between the various social services.

And some accommodation provided is unsuitable. The 'spikes'—accommodation for the single homeless provided by the state—are running far below capacity, despite the fact that they can cost as much as £80 per person per week. The atmosphere in them is generally thought to be too authoritarian to suit the typical dosser, and it would surely be much cheaper to siphon the money spent on these into voluntary organisations which can provide acceptable accommodation for a fraction of the cost.

Despite the activities of many sincere and hardworking people, it is sad to record that the overall number of the single homeless is still growing.

The under 30 age group continue to increase—
symptom of the breakdown of much family life and of
the breakdown of the home town environment.

And the number of women in this world continues to
increase. At the time of the first transmission of *Edna*,
homeless single men outnumbered homeless single
women by eight to one. At a later date this proportion
was reduced to five to one—and now has ended up in a
ratio of three to one.

There is no room for complacency. The problem of
the single homeless is growing faster than is the
machinery for combatting it.

Jeremy Sandford

SELECT BIBLIOGRAPHY

HMSO. *Homeless Single Persons.* (1966).

Holloway, J. *They Can't Fit In: A study of destitute men in St. George's Crypt, Leeds.* London National Council of Social Service (1970).

Lebon, Charlotte. *A Cyrenian Handbook.* The Cyrenians Ltd., 7 Sole Street, Crundale, Canterbury.

O'Connor, Philip. *Britain in the Sixties; Vagrancy.* Penguin.

Parker, Tony. *The Unknown Citizen.*

Parker, Tony. *People of the Streets.*

Reed, Brian. *The Man Outside.* Epworth Press.

Sandford, Jeremy. *Down and Out in Britain.* N.E.L. (1972). *Smiling David.* Calder and Boyars (1974).

Toomey, Lee. *Down and Out.* Waylands (1973).

Trench, S. *Bury Me in My Boots.* London (1968).

Turner, Merfyn. *Forgotten Men.* National Council of Social Service, 26 Bedford Square, London, WC1. (1960).

FILM

The film of *Edna* can be hired from the Cyrenians, 13 Windcheap, Canterbury, Kent.

ORGANISATIONS AND PRESSURE GROUPS

The Cyrenians, 13 Windcheap, Canterbury, Kent.

The Simon Community Trust, Grange Road, Ramsgate, Kent.

The National Association of Voluntary Hostels, 33 Long Acre, London, WC2.

The St. Mungo Community Trust, 34 Abercrombie Street, London SW11.

Christian Action, 104 Newgate Street, London EC1.